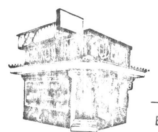

This Book Belongs To:

_____

BROOKLYN BOOK BODEGA

THE CIRCUS ROSE

THE
CIRCUS

BETSY CORNWELL

ROSE

Clarion Books
Houghton Mifflin Harcourt
Boston   New York

✦

Clarion Books
3 Park Avenue
New York, New York 10016

Clarion Books is an imprint of Houghton Mifflin Harcourt Publishing Company.

hmhbooks.com

The text was set in Adobe Jenson Pro.
Art by Jim Tierney
Interior design by Mary Claire Cruz

Library of Congress Cataloging-in-Publication Data
Names: Cornwell, Betsy, author.
Title: The Circus Rose / Betsy Cornwell.
Description: New York : Clarion Books, 2020. | Audience: Ages 12 and up. |
Audience: Grades 7–9. | Summary: A retelling of Snow White and Rose Red
in which teenage twins Ivory and Rosie battle evil religious extremists
to save their loves and their circus family.
Identifiers: LCCN 2019029393 (print) | LCCN 2019029394 (ebook) | ISBN
9781328639509 (hardcover) | ISBN 9780358164432 (ebook)
Subjects: CYAC: Twins—Fiction. | Sisters—Fiction. | Circus—Fiction. |
Fanaticism—Fiction. | Lesbians—Fiction. | Bears—Fiction.
Classification: LCC PZ7.C816457 Cir 2020 (print) | LCC PZ7.C816457
(ebook) | DDC [Fic]—dc23
LC record available at https://lccn.loc.gov/2019029393
LC ebook record available at https://lccn.loc.gov/2019029394

Manufactured in the United States of America
DOC 10 9 8 7 6 5 4 3 2 1
4500796589

✦

For Kathrin,
beloved sister

The two children loved each other so dearly that they always walked about hand in hand whenever they went out together, and when Snow White said, "We will never desert each other," Rose Red answered: "No, not as long as we live."

— "SNOW WHITE AND ROSE RED," THE BLUE FAIRY BOOK, EDS. ANDREW AND NORA LANG, 1889

PLAYBILL

꒰꒱ ꒰꒱

IVORY, stagehand.

ROSIE, acrobat. Ivory's twin sister.

"MAMA" ANGELA, founder and ringmistress of the Circus
Rose. Ivory and Rosie's mother.

TAM, magician.

VERA, strongwoman.

TORO, chief clown and circus accountant.

APPLE, stage manager.

CIARAN, dancer.

BONNIE, contortionist.

BROTHER CAREY, abbot of the Brethren Church.

LORD BRAM, a courtier. Ivory's father.

TOBIAS VALKO, a sailor. Rosie's father.

MISS LAMPTON, headmistress of the Lampton Girls'
School of Engineering.

DIMITY, RACHIDA, CONSTANCE, FELICITY, and
FAITH, students at Lampton.

BEAR, a bear.

THE CIRCUS ROSE

1

ROSIE

And now!
Ladies, gentlemen, and Fey!

IVORY

Rosie and I are twins, but half sisters.

It happened just how you'd guess, of course. Mama loved two men at the same time, and she slept with them both in the same month.

When our fathers wanted her to choose between them, she left them both before she even knew that we were coming.

We might as well have the same father, though, for all we saw of either of them as children. Two absent fathers are the same as one.

But they're different men, and people do insist on being shocked.

Mismatched, half-sister twins are one thing. But our mother *also* being a bearded lady who had worked in what she lovingly called "the freak circuit" ever since she was a wispy-whiskered lass of fourteen years old?

We're circus through and through, Rosie and I. We never had a chance, not a chance, to be anything else.

Rosie's born to the performer's life, though, in a way that I never was. I think she always feels a little cold without the heat of a spotlight on her skin. When she walks the tightrope with her arms outstretched, that wide, easy smile on her face, it's as restorative for her as sunbathing. She floats between trapezes like a mermaid through a sunny sea, without a thought that the air would let her fall. And even when she's simply dancing . . . oh, she shines.

She shines, and the world basks in her light.

I stick to the shadows.

I switched teams, stepped out of the spotlight, and became a stagehand as soon as I realized I could. Mama, thank goodness, was kind about it. She killed off her double-act dreams without complaint, at least to me, and she asked the stage crew to show me the ropes, in both senses of the phrase.

So I got to be behind the spotlight, and Rosie in front.

Even then, of course, we shared it.

ROSIE

Children of all ages!
Ivory and I
are twins, but
half sisters.

You might call us
a sideshow act.
            Presenting,
But here's a
truth, and no
mistake:
            for your
            entertainment and pleasure:
a great performer
is a double
act
            The Rose of the Circus Rose!
all by herself.

IVORY

By the time I was old enough to hold on to memories, Mama had assembled a troupe of about a dozen performers. She'd always wanted the Circus Rose to grow, to become the biggest act of its kind on the three continents.

There was no crew, though, just her and Vera and Toro, frantically stage-managing between their own acts. Everyone worked triple duty as cast and crew and babysitter for Rosie and me: we played and ate and slept under the watchful eyes of contortionists, conjoined twins, albinos, acrobats, equestrians, lion tamers, clowns, dancers.

Finally, in exhaustion, in desperation, Mama admitted she needed a stage manager.

The circus had set up in Esting City, but Mama had been forced to shut down performances when, after opening night, religious protesters blocked the ticket booth. Exactly which part of the circus had offended them was never clear when Mama told the story later, but when she and Vera went out to confront them, things quickly became physical.

No one has ever told Rosie and me the extent of what

happened. But a Brethren priest in the crowd grabbed Mama by the beard and would have —

I still don't know. No one will say.

A huge man who had hoped to buy a ticket for the show got between Mama and the brother. When the priest still wouldn't let her go, the man pulled out a knife and cut her free.

The big man's name was Apple.

"It took me months to grow my beard back," Mama always said. "I only forgave him because of what else I might have lost if he hadn't been there. And because of all he's done for us since, of course."

Apple would always duck his head when she praised him, when anyone praised him, to hide his smile and his ruddy cheeks. He was the first person I ever met besides myself who was *quiet*. Is it any wonder, in a circus?

Apple was a carpenter by trade. He offered to help Mama and Vera repair the ticket booth that had been damaged in the protest.

When the circus left town, he left with us; nothing to keep him at home, he said. He became the stage manager, the foreman of a crew that slowly grew along with Mama's roster of performers.

I admired him: his silent strength, his bashfulness. I started following Apple around backstage as soon as I was old enough not to get into mischief, which was earlier for me than for Rosie.

I watched him and the crew building their sets and handling the ropes, and I learned to help them.

I wanted to build things, to stay behind the scenes, like Apple did. I think he was the first person I'd ever seen who found a way to shine outside the limelight.

ROSIE

Mama started
her circus
without us —
so she thought.
Double pearls,
someday girls,
held blood in
her belly,
while we
waited in
the wings.

Mama, lone,
both lovers gone,
found a new
dream to romance
instead: a circus,
a living, a life.

She hired Vera
first, strong-
woman from
the freak
circuit they'd
both worked
as just-past
girls. As women,
they had found
lives far apart.

But Vera always
says time
doesn't matter,
nor distance, to
a true friend's heart.
Hers remembered
Mama right away.

(And Vera's name,
don't you know,
means the truth.)

What a glorious start
to a circus of roses:

a bearded woman and one
who can throw,
without the slightest
effort, any
man to the ground.

By the time
we made
our presence known,
Mama had Vera
and Toro, too,
the brilliant clown
who was more
brilliant still
with the books.

A business born
with us, a triplet
who shares
my name. More
like me than

Ivory,
the sweet, quiet
sister who thinks,

only, always,

in straight

lines.

IVORY

When I was fourteen, the same age Mama had been when she ran away and joined the circus, she let me enroll in the Lampton Girls' School of Engineering outside of Esting City. I'd been pulling things apart to see how they worked ever since I was old enough to control my hands, and at that school, girls and women of all ages came together to learn the workings of machines for themselves. I had dreamed of becoming an engineer all my life, and the story of Nicolette Lampton — Mechanica, the girl inventor who'd won our king's heart but chose to open the Lampton School instead of becoming his queen — had enchanted me ever since I'd first heard it.

A circus is all about illusion, wonder, people lining up to see something impossible. For most circusgoers, wonder is the goal.

For me, it's the beginning. All the illusions ever did was dare me to find out why and how.

I longed to be a Lampton's girl, but I was terrified of leaving the circus behind. The truth was, though, I found it stifling. That crush of people around us all the time, the performers and crew and crowds and crowds and again more crowds, and Mama calling each and every one of them family. Mama had room for all of them in her heart, down to every last audience member. She loved them as soon as they entered the fairground or came into the tent. Sometimes I thought Mama's heart must look like a playbill, but I told myself Rosie and I were her headliners.

When I left for school, I wanted for once to headline my own life.

Rosie and I had shared every second of our lives with the entire Circus Rose, not to mention with each other. I had no idea who I would be if I were by myself — not a twin, not a daughter, not part of a crew.

Just Ivory.

The thing is, even my name isn't simply my own. It's a duet with my sister's.

Ivory and Rosie, named for the colors of our hair when we were born.

I came first, with hardly a cry at all, a coily nimbus of white on my crown, a serious look on my face.

Rosie followed two minutes later, squalling fit to break glass, her hair a bright slick of red that Mama thought at first was only more blood from the birthing.

For just those two minutes, we were both alone, Rosie and I. I spent them thinking, and she spent them frightened.

That about sums up how each of us feels about solitude.

Mama had planned to name her baby Rose, boy or girl, after the circus she'd so proudly founded. She did not expect two babies, but when she saw us, she thrilled to the prospect of our double act, picturing the posters already.

She chose our names the same way she would have if we'd come to her looking for a paying gig: she named us what would draw a crowd. She drew an equal sign between us with our names, one that said we were the same even as it showcased our difference.

White-haired Ivory, red-haired Rosie. Gentle and quiet, fiery and bright.

Snow White. Rose Red.

We are different. We are the same.

I dreamed, and was afraid, of breaking free.

But at fourteen years old, standing at the front door of the engineering school, Mama's hand in mine for what would be the last time until the end of the school year, I felt something I had never felt before.

I knew what it would mean to leave my family, and I felt guilty — about leaving Mama, to be sure, but even more about leaving Rosie.

Rosie's never had an easy time in the world, you see, for all the joy she takes in performing. Too much of that light and sound she loves, too much brightness and noise, too much of anything pushing in at her senses for too long overwhelms her, and her mind — it just panics. Her thoughts retreat in on themselves until she can't speak, until she can't understand anything that's being said to her, either.

The only cure for Rosie, once she's frozen in overwhelm like that, is to go somewhere dark and quiet, and to rest there for a long time, maybe hours, maybe a day, with someone she loves. Not ever alone.

Since the day we were born, that person was me — even before then. After all, we shared a womb before we were ourselves. I was always the person who was best at bringing Rosie back to the world, at lying patient and still with her in the dark and breathing slowly enough that she would start to match her breath to mine.

At least, I was best at it until Bear.

2

ROSIE

Bear came
to me
from the north.

We were so
young, Ivory and I,
round cheeked,
baby bellied:
young enough that we
weren't yet ourselves

to anyone else.
"The girls," "the twins,"
two buds on one
branch. Just seven

summers old.
Ivory was only
another me

until the day
a beast came
in from the cold.

At the edge
of the campfire light,
Bear rose.

The troupe,
to the last,
fled.

Even Ivory. Even Mama.
Trying their best
to pull me along.

But I,
I alone,
would not be kept away.

I made Bear

a shy curtsey
at the fire's edge.

Bear bowed in reply.
I held out my small
child's hand.

Bear took my palm
in one great paw
and kissed it

clean. A murmur bloomed
from the shadows around us,
wondering applause.

Mama exclaimed:
"Why, he's tame as a pet!
Just what the Circus

Rose needs." Ever
since, Bear has danced
or played the beast

in all our acts —
though of course,

Bear's and mine

are the best.

My heart still holds
its first sight of Bear:

the looming, warm
weight, dark as chocolate,
lush and sweet.

A warren of fur,
a heavy
embrace.

A body that felt
at once to me
like home,

even though I could see
it was not home to

her.

IVORY

Rosie used to turn old circus flyers into paper crowns for Bear. She'd place them carefully on his narrow skull and then cry when she took her hands away and the crown fell off.

Every night, a paper crown, cut out while Rosie did her splits and stretches, her legs akimbo behind her while her hands fiddled with the scissors. Bear's huge bulk made a brown crescent moon behind Rosie. When we went to bed, Bear would go into his cage, but that was really just to keep up appearances: Bear could work the latch himself, though that was a secret only a few of us knew. Everyone who had been with the circus more than a month knew how tame and devoted Bear was.

Every night I watched Rosie and Bear from across the campfire, until, one night, I couldn't stand it anymore. We were nine, and the circus was wintering down in the Sudlands, where the snow never came. The circles of caravans and tents where the cast and crew usually slept were empty; we all slept under the stars whenever we came this far south. I pushed myself up and stomped across the warm sand.

Vera turned away from her two current paramours to watch

me; the rest of the cast and crew were too busy savoring a little leisure time to pay any attention.

"Here!" I said, snatching the scissors from Rosie and taking another flyer from the snowdrift of them that had just come off of Toro's portable printing press.

"Hey!" Toro cried, but I gave him the sweetest and saddest look I could — the one that Mama was always saying proved I had a bit of showboat blood in me yet — and he smiled crookedly.

"Just the one, eh?" He sighed, turning back to his press.

"I only need one," I assured him, hoping it was true.

I thought for a moment, picturing lines and shapes in my head, and then I folded the paper in half, in thirds, and in half again. I glanced at Bear to gauge the width of his head and cut out the paper's center, then made careful slits and shapes along the sides.

"Watch this, Rosie," I said.

I pulled open the folds with as theatrical a flourish as I could muster. It probably wasn't very theatrical at all (no matter what Mama says, I just don't have it in me), but thankfully my work did the amazing for me.

It was an elaborate crown, with jewels and stars made out of negative space between its peaks and frolicking bears between the jewels.

Rosie gasped with all the zeal of an infatuated audience. "Oh, Ivory, it's perfect!"

She lifted the crown in her strong, callused hands — acrobat's hands, even then — and placed it delicately on Bear's head. When she stepped back, it stayed balanced, as I knew it would. By folding the paper evenly, I had made the design perfectly symmetrical.

"Now," said Rosie with great contentment. "Now she is a perfect princess."

I frowned. "A prince, maybe," I said. "Bear is a boy bear."

Rosie gave Bear a long, searching look. "Bear is a princess. Definitely." She made Bear the same elaborate curtsey that she gave the audiences at the circus.

Bear lumbered up off the ground and arranged his hulking body into the same polite pose in return.

Rosie nodded resolutely, as if that settled matters. "Most definitely."

This rankled something that had been bothering me for a long time, but that, at only nine years old, I was still struggling to articulate. "Rosie, you can't just . . . This isn't the show. We pretend things there. Here, outside the big top, they're — they're not pretend. We're not performing now. We're real."

Mama told me so every night, during the private little bedtime talk that was just for me, after Rosie had drifted to sleep on the wings of a bedtime story. Stories had never been enough to help me slip out of the day. I needed to talk, seriously, about things I knew were true. Facts. How long it had taken to break down the tents; ticket sales; or any little thing that had worried my small, serious heart during the day.

Mama always knew that. Always understood. And when the

scarier acts in the circus frightened me, as they often did, she would hug me backstage and ask me to remind her what she told me every night.

"We are what's real," I'd whisper, echoing her.

"That's right, love," she'd reply, the same words every time. "The circus acts are just stories, pretty pretend gifts we make up because we like to give them, to make people happy. But the circus is not the real part of us. Who we are outside it — that's who we really are. Rosie might be onstage now" — for even then, Rosie loved the spotlight and was a born performer — "but who is she really?"

"My sister."

"And who are you, no matter whether you're onstage or no?"

"Ivory. Rosie's sister. Your . . . your daughter." I tried not to hiccup, tried to pretend I was definitely through crying.

"And who am I, first and always and forever? Who is that?"

"Mama."

"That's right. More than anything, more real than anything, my cloud-haired babe. I'm Mama."

And I would nestle into a hug and feel her beard brush my forehead, and I would know exactly what was real. What was safe.

Bear might be a princess or a prince or a dragon or a griffin or any number of dangerous beasties during the show. But here, at the fireside, at night, he was just what he seemed to be. Just Bear. So solid and sure, he'd become one of the cornerstones of my life.

The circus troupe members came and went, Mama adored us but had so many obligations, Rosie went far away inside her mind sometimes, and our fathers never . . .

But Bear was always, always there. And always Bear. Exactly what he was.

I tried to be generous with Rosie, tried to remember how much she liked playing pretend. "Or a king. Yep. My crown is fit for a ruler."

Rosie's lips, I was horrified to see, began to tremble. "Can't you see? Can't you see the princess?"

I felt a knot tighten in my gut. I didn't know why I was getting so angry. "I don't want to pretend with you, Rosie! I made you the crown because — because I knew I could make a better one and I wanted you to have it and be happy, but I won't — I won't pretend Bear is anything but Bear!"

My stomach hurt. My head hurt.

Bear's head cocked slightly to the left. He lifted one huge paw and held it out.

I rushed into his embrace, grasping fistfuls of fur and letting my tears run into the ruff of his neck. "Just Bear, just Bear . . ."

Faintly, I could hear Rosie weeping too. But that just upset me more.

"Over here." I heard Vera's voice, and I knew she'd brought Mama back from our caravan, where she'd been doing design work with Apple.

"Girls, girls, what's wrong?" Mama said, her voice firm and authoritative. "My goodness!"

"Rosie says —" I hiccupped, already embarrassed that I was crying over something so silly. "Rosie says Bear is a princess, and she won't take it back."

Bear rumbled deep in his throat, a soothing sound, and he reached his other paw around Rosie. Mama came and hugged us too, and Rosie and I quieted, safe in the arms of the two beings we loved most in all the world.

Rosie never did take it back, though.

I learned to ignore her. She'd always carried her pretending a little farther than most.

I never did. Never even enjoyed playing make-believe like other children. I think that's why I learned to love building so much and why engineering school became such a precious dream. I wanted to learn how things worked, to take them apart and rebuild them myself, so I could understand the inner workings of a thing just by looking at its outside.

School was the exact opposite of a circus. No illusions. Just facts.

After that night, I learned to keep a place inside myself that was just for me.

Where everything was only what it seemed.

ROSIE

What was the circus like, without Ivory?
Was I some half a thing?

It was never that way. My act
has always been my own.

The first day without her,

true, was hard.

A day on the road.
No show, not even

a rehearsal — just traveling,
earthbound, no open-armed air to
catch me, hold me, make me

live. The first night,

I was sure,
would be harder.

No sister to pillow
my limbs with her own.
Just one fourteen-year-

old girl in a world
all at once far too grown.

Just a floor for a bed
in a caravan
so small Ivory'd called it the Tin Can,

big enough now, my pretty,
to swallow me whole.

After that long

still

day

just as long as a rope that you can't quite

reach —

I found myself standing

outside the caravan,
that single lung,

listening to the open-door
silence turning to one
set of breaths
when I went
inside.

Mama gone
for the night with Vera,
meeting old lovers.

I couldn't bear it,
to sleep
alone that night.

Ivory had a million schoolgirls,
new transplants like her
in a new garden

and I was one Rosie.

I still looked like me, and

in the next show, I'd still be
The Rose of the Circus Rose,
perfect as my posters, but —

it was my roots —

my invisible roots, half gone —

I couldn't bear —

But there was Bear.
Bear in her cage

still play-acting at being
what everyone thought she was.

They thought the cage was locked,
thought Bear couldn't release

the latch with her clever nose.

Bear knows.

I crossed the quiet ground
to the cage

and slipped inside,
not bothering with doors:

a fifteen-year-old wouldn't have fit
but I could, just.

The bars caressed my bones
and I was through.

Bear rose
through the shadows,

slow moving from sleep,
hot as a hearth,

throat-rumbling deep.
Big enough for a girl of fourteen

to hide in. Only just. And besides —
two sets of breath, as soon as I entered.

Tandem breaths.
Tandem hearts, and if one

was ten times my size,

that was familiar, too.

I'd always thought it wouldn't take much
to build a heart bigger than mine.

And the open night air all around us:
the same air Ivory had breathed all day.

Some wind might carry it between us,
the same breath,

a sisterly kiss.
The same breath

she took as she read a book
might pass my lips now, might lift

us through the coming show.
Bear here, and Ivory's air.

I felt myself
blossom and breathe.

Bear lifted one
paw, still half

sleeping, and I fit
myself to earth again,

so tired, I welcomed the idea
of hibernation.

Bear's breath, so long
it matched to every three of mine,

deep as an ocean shell,
deep as a cavern echo

far underground
where the roots hang down.

3

IVORY

My time at the Lampton Girls' School of Engineering was the happiest I'd ever spent, and the hardest. I'd felt such guilt, leaving for that year. I ended every letter I sent Rosie with an apology. When we were small, I used to tell her, lying quietly in the dark, that I'd never leave her as long as I lived. And while she'd released me from that promise long ago, while she'd *encouraged* me to go, I still knew I had broken my vow.

It hurt me almost past bearing.

Guilt over leaving Mama and Rosie clung to me every day, and it came back twice as strong if I forgot them in an hour of rapt studying or an evening of raucous dormitory laughter. I knew tuition was expensive, and I wasn't a scholarship girl; Mama had told me only that she'd handle it, but I couldn't imagine the sacrifices she must have been making to send me to school.

I wrote long letters to Mama and Rosie every week — and though it made me feel a little silly, I always wrote a line to Bear as well, making sure to tell him what I was up to. And I sent my greetings to the rest of the troupe, of course. I was sure Mama read my letters to the group, and even though that made me feel strange, I couldn't quite tell her not to.

Rosie, though, I trusted to keep our letters to herself. So it was in these that I wrote to Bear and that I shared anything that wasn't wonderfully positive; I didn't want Mama to think I was having any trouble at all.

I wasn't having trouble, after all, not really. In some ways, the school wasn't so different from the circus; everyone bonded quickly, though we were all different ages and from far-flung places. I had found friends easily, girls named Dimity, Rachida, Constance, Felicity, Faith — names I stored carefully on the tidy shelves of my heart. The school was just small enough that we could feel like a group, like a tribe; smaller than the circus, and quieter and more orderly, more studious. There were girls as young as twelve, but many were older than I, and plenty of grown-up women came to Lampton's as day students to take classes in building or repairing the machines that made their lives run more smoothly. In many ways school suited me better. But the little troubles, the experiments or the quizzes I failed, the arguments that all teenagers get into now and then and that sometimes hurt more than I wanted to admit . . . those I told to Rosie, not to Mama.

I even had my own bed all to myself. I'd never, ever had that before.

Mama used to keep Rosie and me in the same bassinet, and after we got too big, the three of us slept on the rug on the floor of our caravan together. Mama kept buying props for the circus and upping the troupe's wages, but she refused to buy a bed for herself. She asked us if we wanted them plenty of times, but we had never known anything else, and the rugs and blankets on the floor were more than soft enough for our pudgy children's limbs.

I'd see Mama stretch and wince waking up after a night on the floor with us, though, a problem that got worse as time went by. She tried a hammock made from an old curtain, but gave it up after one night, saying it made her back worse, not better.

So I constructed a plan. I knew what I wanted to do for Mama, and I spent several nights plotting it out, half of another wheedling the stagehands for leftover timber, and a week or two building in secret, in the few spare moments any of us had.

I presented Mama with her foldaway bed on the night of her fortieth birthday, when Rosie and I were going on nine. Rosie, who of course had been in on the plan with me, had collected all the softest, smallest feathers from discarded costuming, and saved up to buy cotton batting to stuff the rest of a mattress that I sewed from faded, but still strong, tent canvas.

When we gave her the bed, she gathered us both in her arms and wept into our hair.

Within a month, her back had improved enough that she could do all her routines again.

But here I go, looping back and back into the past, one memory reminding me of another and another. Schools, beds, Bear, Rosie, Mama . . .

One return begets another, I suppose. And no memory is ever quite as you left it, no matter how carefully you lay it away.

I went to Lampton's, followed my heart as long as I could stand it. But at the end of the school year, I got a letter that made me know I could stay no longer: the Circus Rose was going on a tour to Faerie, and they would be gone, a whole continent away, for two years. Guilt was still eating me up as hungrily as it had done when Mama dropped me off in September. I'd left my twin twinless and my mother with one child (two, she'd say, counting the circus — but even so).

It wasn't as easy to leave school as I had hoped it would be — nearly as painful as leaving the circus had been, in fact. Dimity, Rachida, Constance, Felicity, and Faith tried to convince me not to leave, citing the projects we'd planned to tackle, as if all it would take was a sufficient amount of fun promised in the future for me to stay. I couldn't make them understand exactly why I had to go home. They each had families they missed, but it wasn't the same somehow. School was where they were supposed to be. The circus was where I was supposed to be.

I tried to tell myself that anyway.

I traded our cozy dorm room with its cluster of desks, the quiet evenings where we read and talked about what we wanted to build, and the orderly workroom where every tool had a home for the close-knit chaos of the circus.

I came back full of new skills to share with the stage crew, and we set off on our circuit again, up and down the three continents and then across the great wide sea, to the newly free nation of Faerie. It would be two years before we'd see our home country again.

I missed school and the friends I had made there. But I didn't miss the gnawing heaviness I'd felt thinking of Mama and Rosie — of having left them behind, or of their having left me. After I came back, I made sure to tell both of them every day how much I loved them.

Yet not everything was the way it used to be. Rosie had left the caravan, for one. She slept in Bear's cage, which she'd hung with old curtains and raggedy lace until it was closer to a tent than a pen, the inside strewn with frilly pillows and discarded girlish costumes, her overflowing trunk of cosmetics stashed in one corner and her dressing mirror hanging on the cage door. It had become a favorite joke among the crew that Bear was tidier than my sister.

The Tin Can had ample room for just me and Mama, but the shadows at night made the caravan seem too big and empty without Rosie sleeping next to me. The first few times Mama went out, I slipped away to the cage and slept cuddled with Rosie in the nest Bear made of his body around us. But they had grown toward each other while I was away, and I felt like the third with them. I despised myself a little for leaving Rosie lonely enough to replace me. After that, I went back to the caravan, but whether Mama was there or not, it never felt quite like the home that I'd left.

Mama always said our home is wherever the circus goes, but I'm not so sure.

Maybe Mama is more like Rosie than me. Of the three of us, I'm the only one who always wants my feet on solid ground.

ROSIE

The first time I
stepped into the show,
I knew the light.
The air, applause.

I twirled and leapt
in spotlight gold.
The audience gasped
at a girl so bold.

I chased the bright,
faster and faster to
some white peak that —
as I reached
it burned
away my
balance,
my whole

way to
see —

Ivory saw me stumble
and somehow knew.
She rushed onstage,
straight into the light
she always avoided, for
my sake. She helped me
stagger backstage,
safe darkness,
soft touch. She
stayed with me there.
Our shushing,
matched breaths an ocean
buoying me up.

IVORY

King Finnian was crowned when Rosie and I were only small. He declared that Esting would no longer have an official religion. The new king was full of idealism, and in his first act as ruler, he also turned the magic-filled land of Faerie from an Estinger colony into an independent state. But neither liberating Faerie nor removing the Brethren from court had quite the intended effect. Esting's laws no longer discriminated against Fey immigrants, but many of its people still did, and losing official power had radicalized some members of the Brethren Church. Priests appeared on street corners and standing in open carriages, preaching to the people to turn away from Fey magic and all forms of illusion and accept the truth of the Lord's light. They opened Houses of Light all over Esting City, offering help to the poor and desperate — if they converted. And anything that the Brethren could call deception, from Fey magic to the illusions of the theater or the circus, they were quick to label as sin and to protest.

The Circus Rose weathered many protests over the years, but Mama rarely acknowledged the trouble outside the tent. She preferred to ignore the preaching and praying, the men who stood outside demanding we repent — as if she could will them out of existence.

Most of the time, she seemed to be able to. Their show couldn't compete with ours.

Then, the night Rosie graduated from just dancing and debuted her high-wire act, one of the men got frustrated with yelling from outside and stormed into the tent. Just as Rosie landed, just as the thunder of applause that cushioned her to the ground faded, the man tore in, book in hand, walked right up to her, and demanded she consider her sins.

Rosie had never looked small to me before, not as she did then, the priest towering over her, his face scarlet, gesturing between her and the audience. She looked blank, unsteady on her feet, staggering as she took a step back to put distance between herself and the man. He closed the distance.

The other stagehands rushed out to drag him away, and Mama swanned out with a distraction for the audience, a joke that burned off the haze of his anger, but Rosie was still out there, frozen.

I ran to get her, though I hate being on that side of the spotlight. She leaned against me as I half carried her backstage, where it was dark and safe. Bear was sitting tamely behind the props, waiting for the finale, but he lumbered up when he saw us. I led her to him and tucked her against him, curling up around her too, and together we held her, waiting.

ROSIE

And now,
back to the show.

· 4 ·

IVORY

"Nothing brings the family together like tarot poker." Mama grinned at us from across the circle, stroking her beard.

To my left, Vera laughed. "Just deal already."

Mama shook her head and shuffled languorously. "I so rarely get to have everyone together, that's all."

"Rarely? We've been sailing for a month! I'll be singing praises to my gods and yours when we disembark, just because I'll get to see a little less of you. I'll tell you what I'm looking forward to seeing: a glass of Port's End porter."

"And a porterhouse — a big, juicy steak. I've had enough of fish and hardtack to last me the rest of my blessed life." Toro's pipe sent smoke unfurling around him, like feathers in a showgirl headpiece. Our new Fey magician, Tam, had spelled the smoke so that it was contained in a tight radius around Toro's head, or we'd all be hacking and coughing; the airship's common room was cramped enough, and tonight all the vents were battened down to keep out the weather. We'd risen above an ominous-looking rainstorm just before sunset, but the air above the clouds, while clear, is always freezing cold.

At the start of our journey, it had seemed odd to see so many of the performers not just out of costume, but bundled up completely against the chill. Most of them liked to show off, whether an actual *show* was on or not.

Now we wore our heaviest coats. The airship Mama had rented wasn't exactly first class, and heating was one of many luxuries it lacked.

The troupe had made do, though, as we always did. We'd unpacked tent canvas and curtains to use as extra blankets and to insulate against drafts.

For this game, an old red velvet curtain was spread out under us like a picnic blanket.

"Come on then, Mama, deal us in," Vera continued. "Let's find out what the cards have in store for us in Port's End."

Mama cut and shuffled a final time and, smiling fondly, began to deal us into the game. Everyone else watched each person in the circle as they received their cards, hoping to detect a tell, but I couldn't look away from Tam.

Fe had signed Mama's contract just before we left Faerie, and while fe wasn't aloof or really even all that shy, something about fer seemed more refined than the boisterous circus troupe with whom Rosie and I had grown up. *Something* made fer different, something besides fer Fey heritage — and being neither male nor female, like all Fey — but I couldn't quite put my finger on it.

I caught Rosie smirking at my side, watching me watch Tam. My twin raised her eyebrows and grinned. She had her own opinions about why I thought Tam was special. I could never keep my crushes from Rosie even if I tried; maybe I'd just had so many of them that she knew all my tells. My sister, on the other hand, was never one to fasten her dreams to particular people the way I did. She watched the other acrobat girls with heat in her eyes sometimes, but she never seemed to want to do anything to stoke that fire. She got enough romantic thrill from performing, maybe. She spent her off-hours with Mama and me, or with Bear, when Bear came into the caravan with us like the world's biggest pet dog, as he sometimes did in the evenings or even occasionally to sleep. Rosie always said she never needed to see anything outside of the circus ring or the caravan walls.

Maybe she went so high up in her act that she never felt the need for a wider world, never felt the need to find it in a person.

Tam glanced at me and smiled a little, and I realized I'd been staring again. I snapped my gaze down to the first card Mama dealt me: the Seven of Cups.

Temptation.

Right. Fair enough.

I put Tam out of my head.

"Let me guess," whispered Rosie, nudging my shoulder with

the fluid grace that infused her every movement. "The Magician? Or, no, the Lovers!"

"Hush," I grumbled at her, grateful to have skin dark enough to hide my blushes — and not for the first time, growing up in a household as loud and bawdy as this one. Rosie's pale cheeks, on the other hand, blossom like her namesake flower — only I've never seen her embarrassed. Her face washes pink with excitement and pride when she's performing, so that she hardly needs stage makeup.

Rosie smiled warmly at me. She didn't have to tell me she was only teasing, just like I only had to glare at her to make the teasing stop.

Mama was circling back around to deal our second cards. I tipped my head to rest on my acrobat sister's strong shoulder, and I kept my eyes strictly on my cards until the dealing was done.

"The pot starts at two crowns," Mama said.

We each tossed our coins onto the curtain.

Vera quickly cleaned up on the first round with her set of all four knights, but she got cocky when Mama dealt again, and Tam took the whole pot with fer royal flush.

As Mama dealt us in a third time — more cups for me, just my luck — I got the unsettling *lifting* feeling in my stomach that meant the airship had begun to descend.

Around the circle, we held our cards to our chests and shared excited glances. Outside the circle, I heard glad murmurs and even whoops. In a few hours — just past dawn — we'd touch down in Port's End, Esting's bustling coastal city and the place where Rosie and I had been born seventeen years before. The place where our two fathers still lived; the place where Mama had founded the Rose.

The circus was coming home.

ROSIE

Somewhere in the hold
my love sleeps

under shadow,
through moons.

The wind shifts,
the world lifts,

an old home
reaches up to take us.

Our ship moans
through the turn,

light spilling
through portholes.

Below us whales breach,

heavy, leaping free.

The ship bellies down
to earth. This is

how it is, to feel
something so big

turn its heart
to the sky.

IVORY

We were low enough that I could smell the ocean.

I breathed sea air as we descended from the sky, the airship sweeping down just fast enough that I could still feel the lift in my belly as I watched the coast of Esting rise to meet us.

I let go of the wooden railing and raised my hands above my head, imagining myself leaping down, perfect and beautiful, full of easy grace, like Rosie at the end of one of her routines. An angel touching earth, kicking up the sawdust of the circus ring.

To thunderous applause.

Someone's hand grazed my back.

The touch was warm and gentle, but the surprise still made me jump.

"Happy to be home?"

I twisted around and saw Tam grinning down at me, eyes glinting happily in fer blue-freckled face. Fe hadn't performed with the Circus Rose yet so fe was technically still new, but Mama had hired fer in Faerie over two months ago, and during the long voyage back to Esting, everyone had gotten to know one another — frankly, much better than I'd have liked sometimes.

Especially waiting in line for the baths.

But the circus is like that anyway. You get intimate fast, even though we are a band of itinerants and people join up and break away in almost every city we visit. Cuddles backstage; hugs for good luck; napping in piles in whatever ship or train Mama hired to get us to the next city or the next venue, or around campfires, with the empty circus tents and caravans circling us when nights are warm enough . . .

It's normal for us to touch each other like this. Easy, simple, intimate.

Or it should be.

So I didn't want Tam to know that fer touch made me shiver. "Home? Hardly. I've been a traveler since I was born, you know." I smiled big, wide, and teasing — which would have given the game away if Rosie were there. She always says I'm too serious for teasing to make sense in my voice.

"I know." Tam shook fer head. "I can hardly imagine. But it was in Esting you were born, and it's where your mother is from. That surely means something."

First in the litany of things I'd come to like about Tam: fe was just as serious as me. Even fer magic tricks were performed with all the gravity and precision of a scientist in a laboratory. I loved to watch those thoughtful, deliberate performances, even though I imagined some must find them slow — or they would, if Tam weren't so beautiful. When Mama introduced fer to the troupe, before we even knew what fer act was, I overheard

Vera whisper that fe was so beautiful, she'd listen to fer read scripture.

"Well, home is the circus, wherever we are. Mama's made sure of that. And my father's a noble from Esting City, the capital, although he lives in Port's End now. We write letters sometimes, but I haven't seen him in . . . a while." I took a deep breath as the city came into view. "But still, if I did call someplace home, Port's End would be the top contender. It's where Rosie and I were born, and where the circus was born too."

"Your father is an Estinger nobleman? I thought Rosie said he was from Nordsk."

I felt my lips press together. I had thought a Fey wouldn't ask questions like that. They live in friend groups rather than in couples like Estingers, and one Fey can have many parents. It's one of the things the Brethren missionaries tried to put a stop to when Faerie was a colony of Esting, but it never worked.

Still, maybe all Tam knew of Estinger families was what those missionaries told fer. "Rosie's father is Nordsk. Mine is Estinger. They both live in Port's End now, but . . . we don't see them much. At all." I swallowed. "Mama couldn't choose between them, so here we are. It bothers people more than it should."

Tam touched me gently again, in apology this time. "It doesn't bother me. I have five parents, you know. And one of them is human — a soldier who defected during the war."

I smiled at fer. "I'd better check the luggage again before it's disembarked," I said. "Some of the mechanisms are pretty delicate. I can't have Rosie off-balance for our homecoming show."

"Can I come?" Tam's freckled face lit up. "I still can't understand the first thing about what it is you do, Ivory. The way you make machines that obey your bidding at a simple touch or without touching them at all. It's like . . ."

"Magic?"

We both laughed, and Tam followed me to the hold.

ROSIE

Do you know how to fly?
I do. It has nothing
to do with becoming airborne,

the way Ivory thinks:
so many feathers, this much
tailspin, that much lift.

You can fly in your own
skin. All you need
is to make your hands

rough and find
something strong
to hold on to.

The crowd at the docks
will have such heavy hearts.
Crowds always do.

An acrobat's work
is to lift them too.
Flights you don't see.

We measure the breadth
of each muscle, each breath.
I move them with me.

My limbs could be
heavy as Bear's
and still

I'd bring the sky
down in my grip
and make you

believe
you
too
have
wings.

IVORY

Pink and gold banners unfurled across the starboard side of the airship as we pulled into view of the port. Everyone with free hands had been given cheap trumpets so they could help blare the Circus Rose's tinny theme tune — which made me feel almost grateful for the heavy wheeled boxes I dragged behind me.

I may not have an ounce of showmanship in my bones, but I love being backstage, managing the lights and the music that I'd gotten nearly half automated by then — or better yet, designing some newer, better contraption to show off Rosie's dancing and acrobatics. I was sure the girls from engineering school, not to mention my old teacher Miss Lampton herself, were going to admire the work I'd done. I was going to send Miss Lampton enough tickets to bring the whole school to one of our shows.

Truth was, I should have worked more during the months-long voyage from Faerie. I always think I'll get so much done while we're traveling, but I rarely do — it's so tempting to use the free time resting and reading when being a stagehand demands so much work and so many hours once we arrive at our next venue.

And, all right, maybe I'd spent less time reading on this trip and more time talking with Tam.

But I hadn't had a crush in a long time. It was *fun*.

I told myself to stop feeling guilty, and I refocused on the task at hand: getting the circus on land again and making sure everyone knew we were here.

Mama creates all the fanfare she can whenever we arrive somewhere new; it's free advertising, she says, the gossip about something bright and shiny that's just pulled into town.

I waited impatiently for the end of the showing off, then hurried back to the hold to make sure I could oversee my contraptions getting unloaded in good time.

Usually the Circus Rose does make a fair splash wherever we arrive, with the blaring trumpets and the banners — and we ourselves, of course. Mama has everyone who's willing (that is, exactly all the performers and exactly none of the stagehands) wear costuming and makeup when we get out somewhere new, but we hardly need that to stand out, what with a bearded lady, a strongwoman, a fire-eater, and contortionists and clowns by the dozen among our number. Not to mention the dancing boys, the only group of their kind, and our absurdly beautiful new magician.

Well. Not absurdly beautiful.

Seriously beautiful.

Deeply, gravely, sincerely beautiful.

Black curls tumbling down to big, sooty-lashed gray eyes,

radiantly smooth olive skin constellated with the blue freckles that mark all the Fey. Even the lines of fer nose and chin and cheekbones stroke so lovingly across fer face that they look made on purpose.

Long, slim hands, powerful and delicate at once. Strong, graceful limbs, with a chest you just want to rest against. And a mouth that makes you want . . .

I stopped my own thoughts. I hadn't gotten this swoony about anyone since Mama first hired the dancing boys.

That was two years ago, just before we left on the grand tour that eventually took us to Faerie. I remember the exact day. It was when Rosie and I both knew we were growing up.

We were never permitted to watch the Circus Rose auditions, as much as we begged to do so. We had been allowed to, once, but then a seemingly innocent act turned into something violent enough to give us both nightmares, and after that, Mama forbade it. She and Vera held the auditions, and Mama got final say over the new acts joining the troupe before anyone else got to see them.

It was strange to see the circus tent from the outside on audition days. We were kept occupied sweeping up and breaking down the merchandise stalls and all of those wholesome, boring, busy-making types of things, but despite the rush of activity, there was still an eerie quiet around the main tent: no blaring recorded orchestra, no applause or echoing laughter or unified gasps. Just one quiet phonograph for background music — instead of the elaborate sound system we employed during shows — that was never enough to carry past the thick canvas walls.

I hadn't noticed the dancing boys when they arrived among the other hopefuls in the morning. They would have just looked like . . . like everyone else, then. They wouldn't have put on their costumes yet.

But when the hopefuls walked out of the tent in the evening . . .

I was leaning on the long broom I'd been using to sweep up the path between concession stands. My face felt hot and grimy, sticky with sweat. I was a little out of breath too. I wasn't long back from my year as a student, and I wasn't exactly in stage-hand shape. My heart was thumping and my throat felt a little raw, as if I'd spent the day running laps instead of just sweeping and uprooting tent pegs. It was work, but nothing I would have called hard the year before. I was feeling childish and inadequate and very annoyed with myself for not being bigger and stronger — especially since Rosie had recently had a growth spurt, both up in height and out in some very specific places that made me devastatingly jealous.

Combine that with the fact that I'd already overheard audience members exclaiming over her beauty in a way that was very different from the "pretty child" they used to call her, and I was sure my twin had vanished behind the two-way mirror of growing up and that I had been left behind.

A long parade of unsuccessful auditioners walked morosely out of the tent and drifted away down the side streets.

I carefully didn't look at them, both because no one wants to feel judged when they've already been found wanting . . . and because I was much more curious about the people who'd remained in the tent, who would be signing their contracts with Mama even now.

When Apple nudged me to keep sweeping, I took up my broom again, but I kept my eyes on the tent, waiting . . .

And the boys exploded out.

They laughed and teased and tackled each other and whooped for joy, a baker's dozen of boys — *Well, young men,* I thought — in full stage makeup and the skimpiest costumes I'd ever seen: corsets and thigh-high stockings, some of them, or cropped shirts that exposed long expanses of lean, tight torso, or transparent bits of chiffon tailored as if they were formal suits — except that you could see right through them, skin and limb brushing up against sheer fabric. Some of the boys were tall, some short, some broad and thick-muscled or padded with fat, while others were slender and lithe; all were breathtakingly fit as only dancers can be, every motion of their bodies artful and graceful and deliberate.

I had never given much thought to male beauty before. Outside the tent that day, it overwhelmed me.

I glanced at Rosie, unable even to speak, and I found that she was watching *me.*

She looked . . . puzzled. But before I could collect myself enough to say anything, she just gave a little sigh and a nod, and went off to find Bear.

In the familiar way of Rosie and me, we never had to talk about it; we both already, and in the same moment, just knew —just recognized another of our many differences.

We knew I liked boys in a way that she very much didn't.

In the years since, I'd become a kind of worshipper of male beauty: the swoop of collarbones above flat chests, the expanse of wide shoulders tapering to tidy waists, the vee where stomach muscles meet hips. Thoughtful gazes from long-lashed eyes under heavy brows, the sudden flash of a grin that's just carnivorous enough.

Men were gorgeous. Why women were called "the fairer sex" was entirely lost on me.

And then I'd met Tam, and fe was the most stunning person I had ever seen, and looking at fer and talking to fer sent heat sweeping up through my whole body in a way I recognized from my love of men . . . but fe was no more male than I was. I wasn't sure what to make of that.

Rosie would say I didn't need to make anything of it. She's never felt the need to sort herself into understandable parts the way I do.

Of all the things that people ask me if I envy Rosie for— her easy grace, athleticism, charisma—that fluid self-acceptance never comes up. But it's the one thing I most wish we had in common.

The other stagehands were already unloading, and between their chatter and the heavy lifting, I soon had no more attention left for my own thoughts. I was grateful. Glad, too, that my place in the stage crew meant I wouldn't have to be part of the showy main disembarkation. No one should notice us at all as we trolley-pulled the heavy equipment, hidden behind the performers handing out free samples of wonderment to whoever happened to be at the pier that day.

We emerged.

I'd spent just enough time in the darkness inside the airship that I had to squint when we came back outside.

Besides the bright sunlight that had greeted us as we made berth in Port's End, there was an extra brightness to the warm air. Golden whorls and spirals sparked like fireworks around the airship but made no sound.

Tam herded the lights like a shepherd, murmuring carefully under fer breath and making gentle stroking motions through the air with those elegant hands.

I was transfixed for a moment, until I stumbled into the trolley in front of me.

"Watch it, Ives!" Apple scolded. "I want to live as long as the Lord sees fit, please!"

"Sorry!" I squeaked.

Ahead of us the performers were dancing and sword-swallowing and fire-eating and clowning and contorting, turning somersaults and pirouettes or walking on stilts — and I knew without having to look up that Rosie skimmed the air above all our heads, flitting between the ropes that held the airship to the dock and giving the grandest performance of all. I could tell that just from the faces of the people on the pier, mostly tilted up to watch my sister even though there were so many closer marvels approaching them from the gangplank and on the ground.

Mama's voice, amplified through a bullhorn I'd designed myself and that Tam had augmented during the trip from Faerie with just a little magic, cut clear through the drums and Toro's walking xylophone: "Come one, come all, to the grand and grandiose, magnificent and marvelous Circus Rose, opening Friday night in Carter Park! Buy your tickets from any of our per ... formers ..."

Mama's voice drained away.

I wondered for an anxious moment if my bullhorn design had failed.

I bumped into Apple's trolley again and opened my mouth to apologize — and then I realized that he'd stopped moving because our whole procession had.

The troupe stood still, those on stilts wobbling a little as they found a steady stance, everyone else staring at ... something at the front of our group.

No one on the pier was looking up anymore, either.

I looked up. Rosie dangled by her knees from a thick rope,

and she too stared at something that must be just ahead of Mama. She hung upside down in the air, not even bothering to right herself. And the expression on her face . . .

Well, it told me I'd best be looking too.

I clambered on top of a fellow stagehand's trolley, steeling myself to ignore her grumbles, but even she was too distracted by whatever was up ahead to scold me.

From the top of the boxes, I could see clear across the crowd that had gathered to watch the circus come in. I could see what they were looking at now too.

A show.

Only one that Mama obviously hadn't planned. She'd dropped the bullhorn to the ground, and her mouth was open a little in surprise. The point of her beard trembled.

Two men knelt before her at the end of the pier.

One was brown-skinned with a salt-and-pepper queue, the other pale and red-haired. Both were handsome, the first man slim, the second broad.

The sight of them twisted my heart. I had only seen their faces a few times when I was young, but I recognized them straightaway.

My father.

And Rosie's.

They each rested one arm on a forward knee, and they knelt next to each other, so that their shoulders touched as they lifted . . . something . . . toward our mother. They both smiled at her, and my father was saying something, but I was too far away to hear the words.

Then the ring they held sparked in the sun and the light from Tam's fireworks, and suddenly I knew.

They were asking our mother to marry them.

ROSIE

Oh, my heart —
I usually know,
I'm usually ready —
I can feel it coming, the rush, the overwhelm, the
    crush,
the world turning into too much, and I can back
    away, finish my act, release the ropes, push the
    sky away, be ready be ready be ready for need-
    ing the dark and the quiet and a loving arm
    that will keep me safe, I know who these men
    are, I can't bear it, I can't bear it, I lock eyes
    with Ivory for one moment and she knows too
    and she hates it too but she's grounded she
    always is she always is and I'm pinned to the air
    can't move can't move need Bear — oh lord, oh
    Bear, oh Ivory — sick rushing behind my eyes
    can't move can't move — all black all red all too
    too bright —
oh —

oh.

I feel
my heart
lower. The ropes

lower. I know
the hands
that wait for me below,

the sister's touch,
the grounded hand,
a bird's own
nest.

Oh, Ivory.
You saw me.
Cool hands,
sweet blank.

She saw me.
She saved me.

I open

my eyes to darkness,

fur all along my side,
two shapes in the shadows,
worried, keeping me safe.
Two who love me.
Our fathers outside,

the crowd waiting,
but we are
here.

Alone.

Together.

There's space
to breathe

between
my thoughts again.

IVORY

Thank goodness I looked up. Thank goodness I caught her.

Rosie, hanging frozen in the air.

It hadn't happened that badly in years. Whatever it is that flinches in her mind, the overwhelm that freezes her up, we know the warning signs by now — and we know the things to help her avoid.

But seeing our fathers there on the pier, holding up that sparkling ring; it nearly stopped my heart too.

"Rosie!" I called, rushing to the ropes and ready to pull her down to safety — only these were the airship's ropes, not the trapeze's I had helped design. I didn't know how to manipulate them to get her down.

But Tam saw, and fe was there with me too. One hand still herded fer lights around the circus troupe, and with the other, fe sent a soft current of silvery light up to Rosie, where it cradled her like a gust of wind, like a giant, luminous hand, and set her gently down in my strong arms.

I took her to Bear's berth, where Bear was only just stirring from the hibernation in which he had waited out the trip from Faerie.

Without a word, only a look between us, Tam nodded and left me to my sister and our bear.

I laid Rosie down on Bear's thick fur.

She shivered and began to stir.

· 5 ·

IVORY

Supper that night, without Mama, was a raucous affair.

Not that Mama kept us quiet or even polite — there wasn't much in the way of table manners or refinement of any kind at campfire dinners, which was just how the troupe liked it — but something about Mama's very presence made the rest of us organize ourselves around her, like planets around a sun. Bees around their queen.

Without her, we were just a hive.

"Lord, what's going to happen now? If Mama Angela takes up with the girls' fathers after all this time, she'll want to set up house with them."

"Sure, wouldn't anyone? Those two live in Lord Bram's mansion and I've heard tell even the servants eat off gold plates there."

"The circus is done for. We're nothing without our Mama, and those two will lure her away from us for sure. What right do they have after letting her go for so long?"

In the din, I wasn't sure who said those words, but they might as well have come from inside my own selfish, grasping heart. What would it mean for our fathers to come back into Mama's life? I couldn't even bear to think what it would mean for us, for Rosie and me.

I had never had a father, not really. I had Mama. I had Apple, quiet and thoughtful and capable, and Bear, steady and warm and there every single night if I had a bad dream. How dare two more fathers think they had a right to Mama, to our family?

"I'd go along with just one man that handsome, but two . . ."

There was a ripple of appreciative, slightly shocked laughter.

"You wouldn't think people would be so scandalized anymore, what with the king himself and those two royal friends of his sleeping in the same bed every night —"

"And with more Fey families immigrating every day —"

"Sure, my da's a joiner, and his letters are full of shock at the orders he's had lately, the sheer size of the beds he's been asked to build for fives, sevens, dozens of Fey who want to sleep together. Courtiers, too, who want to mimic the king."

Vera's laugh rang out across the fire. "Mama Angela will be writing to your da, then — she'll need a good strong bed with two braw lads like that to —"

"Vera!" I cringed. "I don't want to hear it!"

She just cackled. Vera had always been that way, bawdy and full of teasing, and usually I liked that about her. She'd been the

Circus Rose's first headliner, the Nordsk Strongwoman, and Mama's best friend since before Rosie and I were born. I knew if Mama had heard what Vera was saying, she wouldn't mind; of all the things to love about Vera, the best was how much she made our mama laugh.

But that didn't mean that *I* had to laugh or to like hearing her jokes. Not then.

Rosie squeezed my shoulder. "Just Vera being Vera, Ives," she said.

I took a deep breath. "Well. What about Mama being Mama? What do you think is going to happen, Rosie?"

She shook her head. "Mama being Mama . . ."

"She always said she couldn't choose, and there they are, *together*. I would never in a million years have thought —"

"Those two will lure Angela away from the circus, clear as the Lord's light," I heard Apple mutter somewhere to my left.

They're going to steal her from us, I thought. And even though Rosie and I have never read each other's minds in the way people always expect twins to do — our minds work far too differently, hers following some kind of pattern I could never decipher if I tried — I suddenly had the feeling that she was thinking the same thing.

That the whole troupe was thinking it too.

Tam walked up, clutching a bowl of the communal stew. Fe straightened fer shoulders and smiled.

Rosie and I both looked up at fer expectantly. I felt my sister's excitement on my behalf rising inside of her — I didn't even have to look, just knew that it was there — and I gingerly pressed my foot down on top of hers, just in case she was planning to say anything unsubtle.

"Hi, Tam," she chorused with me instead.

Our voices are identical, even if the rest of us aren't. It usually startles people when we speak in unison.

Tam, though, seemed unruffled, as fe always did. I wondered if part of fer beauty was simply serenity — then thought, *No, fe would be beautiful even racked with anxiety.* But fer calmness *was* beguiling when my own mind — and the minds of most people I knew — seemed always to be frantically spinning, always thinking too much. Tam's gaze was a circle of quiet.

"Hello," fe said. "I don't mean to interrupt, and I'll go away if you like, but . . . I thought you might want company. Everyone's watching you."

I chanced a look around. It was true; all of the dozens of performers and stagehands at their fires or around the large circle of the central campfire were glancing and murmuring — in the case of the hands — or, if they were performers, outright pointing and staring as they gossiped.

It was easy to tell, just from that, who made their living backstage and who in front of it. When you're performing for the back row, you quickly let go of any inborn subtlety — and anyone who likes to perform doesn't have much of that to begin with.

I rolled my eyes.

"It's the best gossip the family's had in months," Rosie said. "Probably years."

"Probably ever," I agreed, pushing down the slight twinge I felt whenever Rosie called the circus troupe *family*. "There's never been gossip about Mama before."

Tam looked down at fer bowl, and an unbidden, uncomfortable thought crossed my mind: *None that we've heard.*

"Anyway, no one could have imagined such a thing," I said quickly. "Everyone knows the story of our fathers and Mama, and everyone knows —"

My voice hitched so slightly it was impossible that Tam would notice, but Rosie took over for me smoothly, brushing my hand with hers before sweeping it into a dramatic storytelling gesture.

I smiled gratefully, instructing myself not to paint all performers with such a broad brush — some did know how to be subtle.

Not that Rosie, of course, was like any other performer I'd ever seen. Or any other person.

I didn't always understand her, but I loved her. So much.

"We've never even seen them in the same room before. Mama always said they couldn't stand each other. It was going to be pistols at dawn for the favor of her hand . . ."

"So she saved both their lives, and her freedom, and stayed single," I finished, finding my voice again from listening to Rosie's. "She started her own circus and told our fathers she'd never marry anyone. And when she found out we were on the way —"

"Although she only thought she was having one right up until I followed Ivory out —"

"When the both of us came, and the circus grew up as we did, she became more and more sure every day that this was exactly what was meant for her."

Tam smiled. "I like a happy ending. Only . . ." Fe faltered. "Pardon me if this is rude, but something you said seems strange to me. Angela said that if she didn't marry, she would 'save her freedom'. What does that mean?"

Rosie and I looked at each other. "Oh, you know," she said. "Once you're married you can't be with anyone else."

"Tam's Fey," I reminded her. "Fe's used to the big friend-families in Faerie, not to couples." I glanced at the beautiful magician next to me, glad of the excuse to look. "It's not just that, though. When you marry someone your lives are tied together forever."

Tam frowned. "So married people must live together always? They can't live apart?"

I looked down at my bowl. I wasn't sure why, but I didn't feel hungry anymore. "It's not the way it's done. Even the king of Esting, with his so unconventional family, shares his table and bed with his two best friends. If it's not forever, what's the point of being married at all?"

"To be a family. To vow your love for someone and to know that you are loved." Tam nodded at me. "Did you not still have a family, Ivory, in the year you were away at school? And didn't your mother say she wanted you to go?"

I looked down at the ground.

Tam's hand reached for mine and then dropped.

"Mama!" Rosie cried next to me, and I was saved from answering.

Our mother appeared in the ring of light cast by the largest fire. Unnoticed until she wanted to be seen, as always, she nodded and smiled as everyone deluged her with questions.

When she raised her hands, though, the troupe quieted as one.

The ringmistress has that effect.

"I'm glad you're all so interested in me," she said, teasing laughter behind every syllable. "For now, though, I'll keep up my act and continue your suspense a little longer." Her voice softened. "I'd like to speak to my girls, and then I'll go to bed. To *sleep*," she corrected herself quickly when Vera hooted. "Ivory, Rosie?"

We stood.

I walked quickly to Mama and took her hand; I'd heard the weariness and doubt behind the performative gaiety in her voice.

Rosie had heard it too, but she helped in a different way. She turned and walked backward toward the row of caravans, giving an elegant little curtsey to the watching troupe. "We'll get the news out of her, honeys, not to worry. And don't think we don't know what a party you'll have once we good children are tucked up with our toy teddy!"

That got a good laugh. It was true that the grown-up members of the troupe would get up to things once Rosie and I were asleep they didn't even gossip about.

But the better joke was what she'd said last.

No one who'd ever seen Bear could mistake him for a toy.

Bear draped like a shadow over the whole narrow back end of the caravan. His hind legs were tucked against the dresser drawers, the top of his head squashed against the curved wall on the opposite side. In between, his great bulk rose halfway to the rounded ceiling. Dried herbs that kept the air fresh, a few wind chimes, and ribbon charms from Faerie dangled down.

Bear stirred as we entered, not quite rousing. He opened one eye and saw us, then rumbled in pleasure and lifted a front paw.

Rosie dove into him, burying herself between those gigantic furred limbs, each paw the size of her head. She acted as if they'd been apart for months instead of hours.

Bear rested his long chin against her forehead. They both sighed in contentment. My sister looked like a small child again in Bear's arms, like the children we'd been when Bear walked up to our troupe's campfire as purposefully as if he'd come there to audition.

I nestled into him too, leaning against his side, and Rosie draped her legs across my lap. I hadn't realized I'd grown a bit cold at the campfires — nothing really seemed cold after the month we'd just spent in the air — but now Bear's warmth radiated through me like a living furnace.

This was just what I wanted — just us and Bear. Rosie and me and Mama, and Bear loving all of us, Bear keeping all of us warm. We didn't need anyone else — we didn't really need the circus even.

We certainly didn't need two fathers.

I couldn't look up at Mama, couldn't stand to find out what her face would tell us. Seeing the ring our fathers held up, the matching hope and longing on their faces, had been painful enough.

"Well, Mama?" Rosie asked, speaking for me, as always, when my voice was gone. "What's going to happen now?"

Mama took the ring out of her pocket and held it in her open palm. She turned it over, thoughtfully, and something strange happened.

The band, which I had thought one solid piece of gold, split in two. The ring was hinged at each side of its stone's setting — two bands, not just one.

My inventor's heart thrilled a little in spite of myself, and I leaned forward.

"I thought you'd admire it, Ivory," Mama said, handing the ring to me.

I turned it over. The setting held a deep red cabochon ruby as smooth and shiny as a drop of blood. The bands were slim and dainty, but I could still see the tiny letters of my father's initials carved into the inside of one, and Rosie's father's in the other.

I rotated the bands, admiring the delicate work on their hinges. They moved all the way around the stone, and when I joined them together again, I saw that the setting was doubled too; on its other side was a filigree snowflake set with small, perfect diamonds.

"It's beautiful, Mama," I admitted, handing it back.

"It's you two, see? The ruby and the diamonds . . . and their promise as good as gold, they said, that they'd never make me choose again. They want us all to be a family: Bram and Tobias and me and both of you. They'd come with us on tour if we wanted them, and when we're in Esting, we can live at Bram's estate." She shook her head, looking down at the ring, her face exactly like someone in an audience who's not sure if the show is using real magic or tricks.

Bear grumbled, half growling.

"What Bear said," said Rosie.

I took a deep breath. "I don't know enough about them to know what I think. It's — it's strange. I used to dream . . ." *I used to dream of having a father, a real father living with us and loving us, and a home, a place we could always come back to. We both did.*

But Rosie and I had put those dreams away a long time ago, put them so far away that I couldn't even speak them out loud anymore. When Bear had come to us, I'd buried a lot of my wishes for a big, strong, gentle male presence in his thick, dark fur.

I don't know what Rosie did with her dreams. I've always known Bear meant something else to her than he did to me.

"I know, darling," Mama said, stroking my hair. "I haven't decided anything, and I want to be very clear about that with you girls. I told them I need time to think before I'll even know what questions I want to ask . . . I made them promise not to come to opening night, to give me a little space. We've all . . . changed, so much, in these many years. I'll have to get to know your fathers again before I can make any decisions. They hurt me very much once, and I . . . I hurt them."

Rosie and I didn't look at each other, didn't even move, but I felt our matched surprise. Mama had never said before that she'd hurt them, the distant fathers we'd seen so few times in our lives. They had hurt her so much, we'd always known, that she couldn't even bear to bring us to meet them when we were in Port's End before. Vera or Toro or Apple had always taken us, and Mama had never asked a single question about our fathers when we returned — how they were doing, how they looked, what they said. It hurt us both in different ways, I think, Rosie and me. Not to be able to talk to the mother we loved about the fathers we barely knew. But as far back as I can remember, we both wanted to take care of Mama — and we had each other to talk to. So we didn't press her about it.

Mama shook her head as if trying to clear her mind. "But

none of the ways we hurt each other matter as much as *you* do. You two are my family first and forever. We are what's real." She took a breath. "The circus is forever for me too. But if they're only looking for third billing, well . . . I wonder."

"*Can* you even love them again, Mama?" Rosie asked, stealing the words from my own lips. I wanted to add: *Can we? Can Rosie and I ever love these men we barely know?*

But I was too afraid of learning the answer to ask that question out loud.

Mama moved the ring between her fingers, the stones sparkling white and red. She closed her eyes for a long moment and then looked at the two of us, at Bear, and around at our small caravan.

"Never as much as I love you," she said.

ROSIE

The human heart
is a resilient beast.

IVORY

I was awake in the cold, blue half-light before dawn the next day, swallowing coffee brewed in the ashy coals of last night's campfire with the rest of the stage crew, starting work on all the innumerable tasks of an opening day. I was glad of the eye-wateringly early rise, the rush of hard physical work. They helped to keep fathers far from my mind.

I was itching to start on the new props I was designing. Those would have to wait, though, until the tents and vending booths were set up, the sawdust laid down, the mirrors polished, the smoke machines cranked, and the footlights hooked up to the gas supply — not to mention the huge cauldrons of kettle corn popped, Fey floss spun, sausages roasted, and caramel apples dipped. I never got to do my own work on an opening day.

Toro also wanted about a thousand posters distributed all over Port's End. He'd been working through the night already; you could always tell that from the way the tattooed stars under his eyes drooped into dead leaves. Not that much of his face was visible at all behind his helmet of magically contained pipe smoke, but I could see enough to tell that he was in no mood for trifling.

He managed to catch me in the one half moment — just half of one, I swear — in which I'd forgotten my duty and was standing, empty sawdust sack in hand, at the edge of the ring, watching Bonnie stretch and Tam practice fer opening illusion, a rose of white light blossoming between fer hands.

"Make yourself useful, missy, and stop gawping," Toro said, poking me sharply in the leg. He reached up to hand me a heavy stack of posters. "We need these hung in every neighborhood in Port's End before lunchtime, well before!"

I shook myself. "No problem." I draped the empty sack over my shoulder, took the colorful papers, and leafed through them, trying to hide my embarrassment that Toro had caught me "gawping."

Rosie took up the top half of the poster, arching through the air as she reached for her trapeze. Bear reared underneath her, jaws open, looking far more menacing in the drawing than he ever did in life, even during the show — it was obvious to anyone watching that Bear was a gentle beast who loved the limelight as much as Rosie did.

But Mama always says you fill more seats with a little fear.

THE ROSE OF THE CIRCUS ROSE, said curly letters above Rosie, AND HER TERRIFYING BEAR. SEE THEM NOW, BEFORE BEAST CONSUMES BEAUTY!

Smaller portraits dotted the sides of the poster:

VERA THE UNTAMED — here was Vera, barely dressed in a few scraps of tiger-striped satin, flexing her muscles and looking ferocious —

ILLUSIONS FROM THE NEW WORLD — Tam holding a ball of light, gazing out from fer portrait with sweetly serious intensity —

A NORDSK GIANT WHO COULD CRUSH YOU UNDER HIS FEET — Comically, just a drawing of a torso —

ACROBATS, CONTORTIONISTS & CLOWNS BY THE DOZEN — Toro turning a cartwheel and lead contortionist Bonnie in a back bend, with the outlines of many more figures behind them —

& THE WORLD'S MOST GORGEOUS DANCERS — a line of high-kicking, stockinged legs, cut off at the thigh, just so that they might *seem* to belong to women —

I laughed out loud. "Toro, you've outdone yourself with this one. Every soul in Port's End will find something to attract them here."

"Mm, won't they just?" said Bonnie, grinning at me with her head upside down between her calves.

Vera, who was spotting Bonnie as she stretched, winked. "Why don't you take Tam with you? A little magic would help get those posters up lickety-split, I'd imagine."

I glared at her, resenting her blatant matchmaking even as some tiny part of me squirmed with gratitude. "I'm sure Tam has plenty of rehearsing left to do —"

"I'd love to come," Tam said. I looked over as fe doused the glowing rose between fer palms. "I've seen hardly anything of Esting yet, and that's half the reason I signed on for this season. Would it be all right, Ivory, if I came?"

Fixed with Tam's stunning gaze, there was nothing I could do but nod.

We covered the blocks surrounding Carter Park within an hour; Vera had been right about magic making it easy. Tam harnessed the breezes coming off the ocean, led them up the hot narrow streets, and used them to fly the papers to better vantage points than I, or even fe, could reach.

As we ventured farther into the city, I was glad of the chance to show off Port's End as well — at least, what I was able to remember from the scattering of times we'd lived here, in what Mama had called the "off-seasons," between the circus's tours. That had always been late fall and winter, though, bleak seasons for this coastal city.

Now Port's End was a riot of springtime; pale young ivy slithered up walls like snakes, hydrangeas and lilacs foamed over gates and gardens, and the air felt sweet and bright and wide open in a way it never had in the Port's End winters I'd seen.

"Even the sky looked smaller in the off-seasons . . . Mama called them the 'off-seasons,' anyway," I said to Tam as we walked down one crowded lane. "They hardly came every year, though. A few weeks every three or four years, if that. Otherwise, we've always been on the road, ever since we were babies. Mama rarely feels secure enough to stop working."

"That must have been hard on you."

I shrugged. "Hunger would have been harder. And Mama never worked *us* hard. It's just that Rosie and I both happened to grow up wanting to work in the circus too."

"Did you?" Fe looked at me, steady and serious. "It's just sometimes, the way you talk about your year at school . . . well, it seems you'd rather be back there, studying, than working the stage."

I felt my shoulders hunch up defensively, and I made myself shake them loose. "I wanted to study *so that* I could do this better. I'm delighted to be back." I heard a tram coming and turned quickly toward it, not wanting to meet Tam's eyes. "Here, we'll get to the town center faster."

Fe followed me onto the car. I paid our fares and sat down, looking out the window.

Tam sat down beside me, and I flinched.

I was being absurd. I'd never been shy with Ciaran, the dancing boy I'd shared a few months' dalliance with last year, or with any of the one-night flings I'd had with locals as the circus made its rounds.

It wasn't Tam's being Fey that made fer different, or fer extraordinary beauty either. Tam felt special in some undefinable, significant way, and that specialness made me nervous. Made me, to be honest, afraid.

I turned toward fer and forced myself to smile — a task made easy when fe smiled hesitantly back at me.

"I'm sorry, Ivory," fe said. "I was just curious. I can tell you love the work you do as much as I love mine. It's one of the things I like so much about you — your passion."

I blinked. It felt strange to hear Tam say that word, *passion*, so softly and gently.

Fer gaze locked with mine.

The tram began to move.

I looked away. "Well, I do love it," I said. "There's a lot more involved in getting ready for a show than the audience — or even a lot of the performers — realize. The stage crew's work starts long before the lights go up . . . and we're in charge of the lights too. Everything from washing and setting up the tent walls, to the kind and quality of sawdust on the floor, to repairing the benches the audience sits on, to rigging the trapezes and tightropes and curtains . . . we do all of that. And that's what was always the real magic of stagecraft to me. Not performing. All the things we do that, if we're skilled and lucky and pull them off just right, vanish into nothingness as the show begins. All the shadows that no one watches while they're busy staring at sequins and colored lights and beautiful bodies — those shadows are the real show."

I paused and looked out at the terraced buildings lining the road. Close to the port itself, they were mostly storefronts, changing as the tram climbed up away from the ocean from fish-mongers and airship mechanics to greengrocers, bakeries, and clothing stores. At the crest of Port's End's tallest hill was the white marble cathedral, glittering like a lighthouse and visible even from far out at sea. All of it felt familiar and strange, like a relative I hadn't seen in years opening their arms to embrace me.

I ran a finger over the window glass. "When I stand in those shadows, making sure no matter how tired I am that even my breath is silent . . . then I'm the magician. Then I'm happy."

"So you and Rosie really are a double act," Tam said.

I felt something warm up inside my chest. "The whole circus is a double act," I said. "Nothing operates alone. Take the airship we came on or the tram we're riding now — it wouldn't move without its engine, and the engine would be useless without something to move. The wheels need their tracks, and you wouldn't lay tracks if there were no wheels to use them, and inside the engine itself even, one gear needs another, one piston —" I stopped myself, aware suddenly that Tam's eyes were crinkling with amusement. "Sorry. If Rosie were here, she'd remind me to calm down when I start ranting about mechanics."

Tam touched my cheek with one soft fingertip. "I think it's charming," fe said. "I think you're charming."

That spun me enough that I couldn't think of another word to say. I managed to look at Tam for only about half a moment before my courage failed me and I slid my gaze back out the window.

The tram was taking us through one of Port's End's more stylish residential districts; sweet, narrow gray townhouses were lined up next to each other like books on a shelf, festooned with ivy and climbing roses and pale wisteria. I used to imagine living in one of those houses, when we were on the road. There was something so tidy and discreet about each of them, even though they shared walls with their neighbors. Surely the houses on these bookshelf streets had interiors as private as the pages of a closed book too. I remembered one with a lilac-colored door that I'd thought was especially perfect, and I wondered if it might be close by . . .

But when I started looking more carefully at the doors, I realized that many of them were papered with flyers. These weren't gaudy, colorful advertisements like the ones for the Circus Rose that Tam and I carried; they were simple announcements, stark black words on a blank white background.

ONE WORLD

ONE LIGHT

ONE LORD

No, they weren't announcements. They were warnings.

"I wonder what the Brethren would say about that?" Tam murmured beside me.

I frowned. "It's them saying it."

"What? No, not the posters — what you were saying about

engineering and tracks and wheels and double acts. That nothing operates alone."

"I truly do not care what the Brethren would say about absolutely anything," I replied with more vehemence in my voice than I'd intended.

"I know." Fe was looking at me in that warm, thoughtful way again, and it was undoing something deep inside me. "It's just . . . I've spent more than my fair share of time listening to the missionaries droning on in Faerie, trying to save my savage soul. And their Lord certainly, as you would say, *operates alone*."

I raised my eyebrows. "You're the most civilized person I've ever seen. They actually met you and still called you savage?"

"What, you think I'm not?" Tam bared fer teeth and gave a quick low growl.

It was a joke, but I still had to grab the tram seat to keep from pulling fer to me and finding out what it would feel like if Tam growled while I kissed fer.

The tram stopped.

We got out, posters in hand.

Tam eyed the nearest Brethren flyer. "I can show a little savagery when I like." Fer hand flicked upward.

A sharp wind whisked between us, and the paper exploded.

Tiny fragments drifted down like snow.

With another small motion, Tam sent a poster from the top of my stack whisking up to the same spot where the flyer had just been. It smoothed itself against the wall, perfectly straight, held up by nothing but air.

"Leave it a little crooked," I said. "Perfection never stands out — people notice flaws much more. That's one of the first things a stagehand learns."

"That can't be right," Tam said, closing one eye and squinting up at the poster with the other, "or I wouldn't have noticed you."

An obvious line. It would have made me roll my eyes . . . if anyone else had said it. Yet I was suddenly lightheaded, and the stack of posters, no real burden, grew heavy in my arms.

Tam twitched a thumb. The poster tilted just enough. Its metallic lettering caught the sun.

We looked at each other.

Fe raised a hand and beckoned, but not to me.

I felt a cool breeze at my shoulders, gentle but insistent, pushing me forward.

This time, as Tam's gaze held mine, I kept looking right back.

Fer hands came up and touched my face. Reverently. As if I were sacred. "Ivory, I want to ask you something," fe said.

I blinked. "Yes?"

"I'd like to kiss you. I know you like — I mean, I know you used to go with Ciaran, and I've seen the way that you watch the other dancing boys, but —"

I laughed, and the sound was huskier than I'd expected. "But you haven't seen the way that I watch you?"

Tam's grin rearranged the constellations of fer freckles, and fe kissed me.

I kissed right back. I'd had plenty of kisses, of course, probably more than my fair share, in my life with a traveling circus. It was true I'd never wanted to kiss the other girls at Lampton's, and before I met Tam, I thought my heart melted for men alone, but . . .

But all of me was melting now. Every bit of my body was going liquid until I didn't know how I had bones left to stand on.

I heard Tam click fer fingers, and the whole bundle of posters rose out of my arms. Fe closed the space where they had been, fer chest pressed close against mine.

The breeze around us grew to a trembling wind.

I tasted sweetness and shadows and heat. A sigh escaped me before I could stop it, a tightness that pulled up from deep in my belly and brushed past my lips to meet Tam's in a low breath that was almost a groan.

And fe answered — in my mouth, on my tongue, and curling in my ears, I felt the slow beginning of Tam's growl.

Savage.

"You there!" snapped a cold voice.

We parted, startled. Tam's lips were shiny with the traces of our kiss, and for a moment, I could not look away from them. But then I looked up at fer eyes, and I saw that they were afraid.

"Who on earth do you think you are?" the voice continued. "This is holy ground! This is desecration!" A robed priest elbowed his way between Tam and me.

I stayed still, although Tam stumbled several steps backward, fer eyes still fearful.

"What holy ground?" I said. "We're on a public street!" I filled with anger, remembering the tender way Tam had touched me. "What desecration?"

"Young lady, you are standing in the doorway of a House of Light." The priest gestured to the gray building before us, a tall, narrow townhouse like all the others on this road — only with a door painted bright white, instead of the softer colors of the others. Now I could see the iron sunburst that hung above it, the symbol of the Brethren Church; the priest wore the same image, but smaller and cast in platinum, at his collar.

"This is one of the Brethren's many charity homes, child," the priest said, his voice icy with condescension. "This house takes in fallen women. We give them employment as laundresses and a safe place to stay and a chance to restore their souls to brightness." He sniffed. "Perhaps *you* have need of our services, or your young . . ."

The priest glanced back toward Tam, and I thought he was just pausing to emphasize the fact that he couldn't call a Fey "young man" or "young woman."

But he frowned and squinted, as if he couldn't see fer at all.

Tam let out a long, slow breath of relief. Fe smiled at me, and for a moment, I swear I saw *through* fer, straight to the cobblestone street. The space where Tam had been shimmered, and fe became solid again . . . at least to me.

A trick of the light. What else could I expect from a magician?

It worked a treat; the priest looked right through Tam as if fe wasn't there.

"Well," he muttered, turning back to me. "How *virtuous* of that Fey to leave without you, and after using *magic*, too," he sneered. "Still, I was a missionary, and I learned the hard way that you can't expect much better from them. Perhaps you'll come in, child, for a cup of tea, and I can show you the more wholesome ways that the young women here pass their time?"

Tam clapped fer hand to fer mouth to smother a laugh. The motion upset the stack of posters above our heads, and a half-dozen of them fell onto the priest's head.

"Sorry, Brother, but I'm busy today," I said. "If any of your fallen women need a bit of a lift, though, they should come see us at the Circus Rose tonight."

The posters plastered themselves against the charity house's door as if of their own free will.

I ran down the street with Tam, leaving the priest frowning.

I wanted to pretend that the propaganda we'd seen on that street was just due to the proximity of the charity house, but once I was looking for signs of the Brethren, I saw them everywhere. Posters on windows and doors, of shops as well as private homes, even a

banner just outside the courthouse. And preachers, too, on practically every street corner as we got closer and closer to the heart
of the city. I knew the Brethren had been mobilizing in Esting
since King Finnian took away their official power, but it seemed
to have gotten much worse in the two years that the Circus Rose
had been touring abroad.

Even the waiter at the café where we stopped for coffee and
sinnum buns had a pendant with the sunburst of the Brethren
dangling on it. He eyed Tam suspiciously as we left.

"He oughtn't to look at you like that. He must get Fey customers every day," I grumbled as we walked.

Tam glanced back. "That doesn't mean he has to like us," fe
said.

I scowled. "Well, we're going home to the circus now. Everyone likes you there."

As we approached the striped skyline of the Circus Rose
tents, though, it seemed that I was wrong. Black-robed Brethren dotted the crowds and lines of people who had come to
see the performance, talking seriously with some and handing
out flyers to others. Most of the flyers had been immediately
discarded, judging by the number that lay trampled on the
already-dusty and path-worn ground. That was something,
anyway.

But as I watched, a few audience members listened to the
Brethren, murmured seriously to one another, and then turned
to leave.

I glanced to our left. We could see the ocean from there, and over it, the sun was beginning to set.

"I'd better get in to help Apple," I said.

"Mm, and I need to do my makeup." Tam straightened, suddenly seeming taller, and fe laughed. "I think what I put on this morning might have gotten a little smudged."

I burned from the belly up. "You look beautiful to me," I said.

Tam brushed two fingers across my mouth and then held them up, showing me the rouge fe'd left on my lips. "See you after the show."

Fe turned and left.

Thank goodness. I wouldn't be able to get anything done if fe stayed with me. And I needed to work.

Plenty of it to be done too: props to check and repair, ropes and gas lines to hook up, sawdust to sweep, Bear's decorative harness to polish and help him put on (he wouldn't let anyone do it but Rosie or me). I had to rush through all my jobs like a triage nurse. That's opening night for you.

As I hurried by the park gate, I saw yet another Brethren preacher standing right there. This one wasn't just any street preacher either; he dressed like an abbot. He wasn't making conversation with a few people like the others — no, he'd set up a show of his very own. He introduced himself to his audience as Brother Carey. He stood on a whitewashed box he must have carried in with him and he projected his voice, trying to reach the whole crowd at once — and doing a fairly decent job of it too. He had the same charisma that good performers have, that compelling aura that makes people want to look at you, listen to you. No amount of makeup or training can fake that, I knew well. Even I found myself listening to him.

"You come here to be deceived!" he said, accusing the audience even as something in his voice suggested that he cared deeply about them. "You know what a circus is: smoke and mirrors! You know what any theater is: falsity! A distorted, lying mimic of true life. If you need proof — if the words of the Lord's emissary are not enough for you — only look for the depravity, the mimicry, the doublings in the shows that you will see here tonight! Not a performer uncostumed, undisguised. Not an act unaugmented by sleight of hand, by distraction and misdirection. The marvelous things you will see here tonight are only marvels because they are lies! And sin, yes, sin of the most shadowy and darkest kind —"

I shook myself out of listening and marched right up to the preacher, my hands clenched at my sides.

"Excuse me," I said. "You're not welcome. We've rented this park for the next two weeks, to do our business here. And you are bad for business." I pointed at one of the MANAGEMENT RESERVES THE RIGHT OF ADMISSION signs scattered around the fairgrounds. I realized that my hand was shaking, and it occurred to me that I was still angry with the priest who had scolded Tam and me that morning. In truth, I was angry with every brother I'd seen since we arrived.

To find Port's End invaded in such a way, the closest place to a home that I remembered —

It stopped with my circus. I wouldn't let them invade this too.

I felt my guts twist. The Brethren hugely valued Estinger-made technology — they'd been the most powerful patrons of the industrial revolution that had come a generation ago, after the last king had outlawed all magic. Esting had depended so heavily on Fey magic for our daily lives — cleaning and lighting our houses, aiding in transportation, all the infrastructure of a society — that we'd had to innovate or die when we were suddenly deprived of such a basic commodity.

And we had: there was steam power and gaslight now, trams in the cities, carriages pulled by lifeless automaton horses, airships, and even, it was rumored, something called a railway that would connect the three nations of our continent in ways we'd never imagined before.

Now that magic was legal again, the number of inventors and engineers had begun to drop. But since the Brethren still considered magic sinful — even though they didn't also get to call it illegal anymore — they put a lot of their considerable money and influence behind libraries of engineering and technology, and even schools to train new inventors.

You just had to pledge fidelity to the Lord to join those schools. And they were only for boys.

I'd have recited any pledge they wanted to get to learn the

things I wanted to know — and I probably would have dressed as a boy too, if I'd thought I could get away with it.

But the Lampton Girls' School of Engineering, while not quite so well-funded as the whole Brethren Church could obviously make their schools, had been the perfect fit. They could combine science and magic at Lampton's the way we did at the circus, and that thrilled me. I loved it. It felt right.

The preacher glared down at me from his soapbox. He wasn't a remarkable-looking person at all, really: stodgily built, of average height, with the shaved head that most higher-level Brethren shared. That did surprise me; I always heard that those higher up in the Brethren's chain of command lived lives of sequestered luxury in their abbeys.

With this man, though, it seemed to be a matter of passion rather than assignment.

"All the face of the earth is under God's purview, child. Doesn't His light touch the ground here, even now? As an emissary of that light, I am only reflecting His."

I pointed west. "The sun is setting."

I felt someone yank me backward — and none too gently, either.

I turned; it was Mama.

"Hey!" I protested as she dragged me off. "What are you doing? I'm trying to help! That man is driving away customers!"

Mama eyed the preacher and those gathered around him. "Is he?"

I looked again, and after a moment, I saw them. Toro and Vera were weaving through the edges of the crowd, selling tickets — although most listeners stayed for only a few minutes, then made their way straight to the ticket booths. When he said something absurd about the extreme sinfulness of our show, a whole dozen or so of his listeners made a dash for the main booth, digging in their pockets or purses as they went.

"We could have no better advertising than what that pompous ass is giving us for free," Mama said. "Let him stick around. He's doing us a favor."

I had to agree. "But, Mama, there's something that bothers me about him. It's like he's a — a wrench in the works of the circus. It feels like he's hurting us when I hear him say those things."

"Him?" Mama scoffed. "Couldn't hurt us if he tried. It's like I said — the more he tries, the more he ends up helping. Don't give him another thought, honey love."

But I gave Brother Carey and his henchmen plenty more thoughts as I set up for opening with the rest of the stagehands; I just kept them to myself.

I was running back to double-check the gas lines when I heard someone in the dressing room tent give a despairing, theatrical wail. I met Apple's eyes, we both sighed, and he waved me toward the wailer while he ran toward the footlights. I was better at soothing preshow jitters than he was, and we both knew it.

By the time I'd rebuilt Bonnie's ego and rushed backstage, the tent doors were closing, enveloping the audience in shadow that made them hush their laughing chatter and turn from a multitude into one silent, waiting presence. I had managed to mostly forget the Brethren and all the half-done or undone jobs that fall in the wake of every opening night — I'd forgotten everything but the job in front of me, the rough feeling of the rope in my hands as I worked in tandem with Apple to shine the first spotlight.

The show was about to begin.

· 6 ·

ROSIE

I render the air —
tent-peak shadow, lush darkness —
dip my toes in the lights, soak my limbs, drench
   their eyes.

Spin down from the center and leap for the edges,
my red skirts, white smile, black heart in plain sight.

I show them the shapes
that they don't know to dream of,
I dance on steel wires and balance on light —

I'll be the one girl they can think of, see, long for,
sweep into their gasps and their dreams and their
   sighs.

My Ivory has built me
high wires, trapezes,
the sturdy, strong ground that launches my flights.

When I fly, I don't shake, I don't stutter. I'm no
     stranger.
Every face in the crowd's a heart I recognize:

A moment of union, transcendence, elation.
A brief lifting free
from the fires
of the mind.

IVORY

Rosie was always our showstopper. Nobody ever wants to follow her act, so she goes last before intermission and then second to last, with Bear, before joining in the grand finale. I always loved to watch her — and I always worried about her until her act was safely over, no matter how many times I'd seen her execute it perfectly.

Still, I wasn't impatient as we swept through one performance, then another; I was kept plenty busy as a stagehand, of course, and then I still loved to see all the acts, even the ones I'd seen a thousand times before. Maybe especially those.

First was Mama in her red jacket and top hat, playing mistress of ceremonies and telling teasing, just-bawdy-enough jokes to make the audience laugh and relax. Toro and the other clowns were waiting in the audience to reveal themselves at choice moments in Mama's monologue, to sweep and leap and dance and somersault down to the stage and make the audience feel that they too might be part of the show. To blur the footlights' line.

Next came the dancing boys, our opening act ever since they'd joined us — and a wise choice too, an inspired one, really, from Mama. Between the thirteen of them, they seduced everyone in that tent. I used to think they were the most beautiful people in the world . . .

I'd been wrong on that score. Even the memory of Tam's kiss sent a searing shiver through me.

But I still liked to watch the boys dance. Ciaran especially — we'd been each other's first lovers, and while we shared only an easy friendship now, it still made me smile to see him move his hips with such grace and cast the same fetching glances at his enraptured audience that had once seduced me.

It was extra fun to watch from backstage too. Many of the men in the audience had never looked at another man the way Ciaran and the dancing boys *demanded* to be watched.

That was one of the things I loved most about them; most women had never been offered male beauty and bodies on a platter that way before, either. Girls are used to gussying up, trying to look pretty and appetizing and generally like something edible, something for men to devour until nothing is left.

That's part of what I hated about performing, even as a child. The look on the faces of certain people — certain men — in the audience that you can't describe in any other way than *hungry*.

It's what most of the more risqué circus acts have in common, something that undercuts every show and that everybody knows, but they know it so deep that they don't think it's even worth talking about.

Women perform to make men hungry.

Men watch to eat.

The dancing boys flip that deep-down knowledge neatly on its head in their first moment of performance. Men see bodies like their own offered up for the pleasure of . . . well, everyone. Anyone at all who has an appetite. Then they maybe start to sense a hunger of a different kind than they've let themselves feel before.

And the women, even the married ones, are too often like I was that hot dusty day when I first saw the boys leave the tent — they're waking up for the first time to the fact that, their whole lives through, they've been *starving*.

After the last swooping, languorous blare of the trumpet in the dancing boys' act, there was a moment of silence and darkness — the liquid shifting darkness that lets one act flow away and then reveals the next act in its place in the center ring.

The second act was Tam and fer illusions.

Fe performed gracefully, slowly, sending glowing whorls and spheres around the tent in an intricate dance, seeming to pull some from the mouths and eyes and chests of certain members of the audience, all different colors, all merging and shimmering together overhead and out to the very cheapest of seats in the back. Tam told me on the trip from Faerie that fe always tries to give the cheap seats the best show of all, since that was all fe could afford the first time fe went to the circus.

I felt close to overflowing with how much I liked fer in that moment. Something trembled along the edges of my body like water about to spill over the lip of a glass. I liked everything fe was doing and how fe was doing it — that fe was also so beautiful while fe was being wonderful was almost an afterthought.

Almost.

"Making yourself useful, Ives?" Apple whispered from behind me.

I turned. He had a strange look on his face, like he was fighting with himself, not like he was checking on one of his stagehands.

"Everything's under control. I had a spare moment." I tried not to blush.

"You should be careful." He paused, chewing on his lip. "Tam means well, but fe is what fe is."

I stared at Apple. He couldn't mean what I thought he meant. "Because fe is Fey?"

"Because magic isn't safe. You can't trust it. You don't know where it comes from or what it can do." He looked toward the crowd. "I told your mama, I don't think there's any place for magic in the circus, but she's always one for trying new things."

"We've always had magic in the circus."

"We've always had tricks. But you know as well as I do that tricks make sense when you're on this side of the curtain. Magic never makes sense." He sighed quietly, turning to go back to work. "You just think about what I said, okay? It's important to know what's real."

I didn't want to think about what he'd said. And thankfully, the following three acts required so much of my attention

—pulling ropes, pushing levers, changing light colors, minding the phonographs that produced some of the sound effects—that I didn't really have to.

And then it was time for Rosie. Even in the rush of everything I had to do, I loved seeing her perform too much to keep working while my sister danced. I stood back, just beyond the edge of the pool of light in the ring, ready for Rosie's acrobatics to unfold. We'd set up the high wires before the show started, so now there was nothing for us to do but watch.

Rosie descended from the shadows at the top of the tent, her gold costume glittering with sequins, a flowerlike spray of pale pink feathers arranged at the back of her auburn updo. More gold sequins adorned one eye and cheekbone, as if she'd crashed sideways into a star on her way to the stage.

She perched like a bird on her trapeze, holding the rope and lowering herself slowly until she was at the exact midpoint between big top and sawdust, suspended in the air at the center of the circus universe.

The Rose of the Circus Rose.

She showed the rope she used to lower herself to the audience, winked, and then let it go.

She flipped upside down on the plummeting trapeze.

The audience gasped as one.

Then—thanks to one of my own designs—an invisible catch stopped the rope in its tracks and the trapeze halted just in time.

The feathers in Rosie's hair brushed up sawdust on the ground in a cloudy halo.

She lightly flipped again, landing smoothly, smiling her radiant-sun smile at all the world.

Relieved laughter and applause.

She waved, still smiling, and spun slowly all the way around, giving that warm look to everyone as she went, so that suddenly each person who came to see the Circus Rose felt as if they were the star of the show too. They felt seen.

This is a different kind of hunger than the dancing boys evoke — although I know that gorgeous Rosie breaks more than her share of hearts too.

But once she's gotten everyone on those benches to fall in love with her, what she gives her audience — above and beyond her breathtaking aerial dance — is the feeling she's loving them right back. It's why Rosie gets more flowers thrown at her feet, more admirers lining up after the show, more letters sent to our traveling group even years after the writer's day at the circus, than anyone else of our number. She doesn't just inspire love — she gives it, with every movement of her act. I often wonder if that's what exhausts her so profoundly that she has to hide with Bear for half a day after every show, what makes her mind hurt so much that she vanishes inside of it sometimes. All that giving.

They could just watch her forever and be happy, I thought, looking out at the rapt audience, *and so could I.* Glowing pride and love for her was filling up my whole chest when I caught the sinnum scent of a newly familiar perfume and realized that Tam had come to stand beside me.

Fe was still in full stage makeup: heavy-handed, smudged eyeliner, as if fer eyes weren't dark pools of honey as it was, and a trace of silvery shimmer on those high cheekbones, that arched nose, the cupid's bow of fer perfect mouth.

"Hello, Ivory," fe murmured in the under-the-breath voice everyone uses backstage. Fe stroked fer hand lightly along my arm in greeting.

I could watch Rosie forever . . .

But I'd watched her before.

I shivered under Tam's touch and turned away from the ring.

"Hi, Tam." I took fer hand where it was lingering at my side and weaved our fingers together. "Do you think you can make us both disappear?" It was dark backstage, true, and I had no responsibilities for the next few minutes, but I still didn't wish to make a spectacle of myself. I never did.

"Mm," Tam said. Fe waved two fingers delicately through the air.

We smiled at each other, and the smiles were a secret.

I was grateful for every touch I'd known before, for every kiss, because I knew what I was doing when I pushed my other hand through Tam's thick hair and pulled fer roughly in for more of what we'd had that morning.

I only surprised fer for a moment. Tam's hand tightened around mine and our bodies pressed together and fe pushed me against the large pulley behind us. The metal and thick rope dug into my back, but I was too focused on the taste of Tam's mouth, the feel of fer lips and tongue and teeth.

The kiss went on for long breathless moments, our bellies pressed together and Tam's legs pushing between mine, fer body all against me, and the cold, hard metal of the pulley at my shoulders. Our fingers tightened together; my free hand fisted in Tam's hair, and fe drew me toward fer at the waist with those long, elegant, marvelous arms.

The whole world contracted. Just the two of us here — no twin, no troupe, no circus at all. The only person in the world for me just then was Tam.

And it was clear as day in every moment of our kiss, every movement of Tam's body, that I was the only one fe wanted too.

It was so lush that I found myself shaking between kisses and touches. I squared my back against the pulley and brought my legs up, wrapping them around Tam's waist. We soared through a blessed, private, heat-soaked darkness. Even the light in the ring turned red with the fire we made.

Tam's mouth moved down from mine, slipped warm and slick over my jawline and my neck, bit at my collarbone —

I was gasping again, breathless, not enough air in the world — and a sound in my mind like a rising crowd, like screaming —

Screaming.

No, not in my mind.

In the ring.

We pulled apart, sharing a frightened look.

I still couldn't breathe.

Couldn't breathe for the smoke that was filling the air.

Smoke.

Screams.

Red light in the ring . . .

"Fire!" I shouted, but my cries were lost in the sea of everyone else's screams of panic.

Tam and I rushed into the ring, running almost headlong into Toro and two of the stagehands, who were desperately trying to take down one of the tightrope supports.

I looked up and saw why: Rosie was hanging in midair on her trapeze, an impenetrable haze of smoke above her, the fire painting its evil lights over her face and making her gold costume blaze like a hot cinder.

"Ivory, Ivory!" she called. "Bear!" And then, like a small child: "Mama!"

"I'm here, Rosie, I'm here!" I screamed. "I'm going to get you!"

But even though she was only twenty feet above me, close enough that my voice surely carried, she didn't even look down. She just kept screaming and twisting around and calling for Mama, so that the trapeze rope wrapped inexorably around her limbs —

A fire in the circus could kill her. It was more dangerous to

Rosie than to anyone else because it forced her mind right into overwhelm. She'd gone inside herself, and she couldn't understand what was happening.

"Ivory, we have to get out!" I felt Tam's arms around me, dragging me away.

"No, stop!" I said. "She doesn't understand!"

"Look around you!"

I could barely tear my eyes from Rosie, but one glance showed me burning great shreds of the tent itself collapsing around the ring, ropes falling to the ground like flaming snakes, fire tearing across the sawdust and wood chips in the ring as quickly as if they were made of kindling — which they were.

"Oh lord," I said, "the footlights —"

They exploded.

I shielded my eyes with one arm and flung myself back against Tam, keeping fer under me as we both fell to the ground. Flying shards of glass from the footlights crossed over us, and I heard a chorus of cries of pain.

This was my fault, mine — I was supposed to double-check the gas connections before we let the audience in, and I'd been running late all afternoon, between mooning over Tam's kiss and fuming about the Brethren —

No time for guilt, not yet. I knew we had only minutes left, with the gas from the footlights feeding the fire.

We had a sold-out show. Five hundred souls in the seats.

And Rosie above us only one.

My sister, the one life I'd choose to save before even my own, if I had to. If I could.

Someone loved every single person in the tent as much as I loved Rosie.

But still I couldn't leave her.

I ran to the trapeze ladder and grasped it. The metal was hot enough that I watched my palms turning angry red and blistering as I started to climb, but I hardly felt the burning, couldn't think of stopping until I got to my sister. She needed me, she'd always needed me, and I'd known after that year at school that I could never abandon her again — and by the lord, I wouldn't abandon her now.

My eyes watered from the smoke so I could hardly see, but I climbed.

Then someone grabbed me, someone far stronger than I was, and I felt myself yanked back down to the ground and across the ring. "Let me go!" I kept shouting. When I finally wrenched my gaze away from Rosie, I saw that it was Tam and Ciaran, together, dragging me away. For that moment, I hated them both.

I saw Apple nearby pick up and carry a screaming man with glass lodged in his eye. Vera and Toro were at the edge of the ring, directing the panicked crowd out into the open air as quickly as possible. Other stagehands swarmed around us, carrying audience members who had already passed out or who were too injured to get out on their own.

That first breath of fresh nighttime air, when I finally got it, was like a miracle and a nightmare — as healing to my raw lungs as sleep at the end of a long, cruel day, but a breath I knew my sister could not take. I felt as if her still burning, choked lungs were housed in my body too.

Apple was standing in the field, directing the stagehands to lay out the people who were too hurt to walk. "Lord save us all," he kept saying just under his breath, as if he didn't think his prayer would be heeded.

Everyone outside, troupe and crew and audience alike, did what they could to help the injured. Many people were so badly burned that I could hardly stand to look at them; their clothes stuck to their ravaged skin in the places where both skin and clothes hadn't been burned away.

Ciaran and Tam were already jogging back toward the flames to help carry out more victims.

Then a huge, animate darkness ran past them, like a shadow in a dream. It was Bear.

Running right into the heart of the fire.

A scream bloomed and died in my throat; I didn't know whether I wanted to call Bear back to safety or urge him on in the hopes that somehow there was something he could do for Rosie. If anyone had a chance of getting through to her, I knew well, it was Bear.

He passed by Vera, who was kneeling over someone in the line of the unconscious, a short person in a soot-streaked, singed red jacket.

Mama.

I stumbled toward her, reaching out, feeling just as I had when I was small and had woken from a nightmare and nothing but Mama's arms would make me feel safe again.

But Vera held me back before I could reach her. Her muscular arms bound me as thoroughly as ropes. "Don't touch her, darling," she said. "You'll hurt her. The burns are bad, but they're just on the surface — see how she's breathing steady? She'll be all right. She'll be all right." She took a long, shaky breath. "Angela, you'll be all right."

I'd recognized Mama by her costume, and now, up close, I could see that I'd never have known her face like this: eyes not just closed but swollen shut, and all of the tidy dark beard that had been her first living burned away.

I knew Vera was right that touching her would only make things worse. I had to believe that she was right about Mama not being too hurt, either — I couldn't bear to think of the alternative.

It was true that her breathing was steady.

I nodded.

Vera let me go and crouched over Mama again.

I steeled myself to go back in, and I turned toward the fire.

I saw a painting of a nightmare; more than half the tent was already incinerated, and long red flames were licking up the remaining canvas and support beams in a mockery of the vertical stripes of the tent fabric itself, stabbing bright sparks up into the sweet night sky.

The big top was a skeleton. Where I'd seen Rosie hang in frozen terror a few minutes before, there was only empty space. Where the trapeze had hung, I could see all the way through to the sky.

I scrabbled toward it, and Tam was there at my side, trying to hold me back. But fe's a performer, and not even a dancer like Ciaran. I'm a stagehand and much stronger, and I wrestled out of fer grip with ease.

I ran a few good steps before someone caught me again. Apple this time.

The skeleton that was the circus tent collapsed into flaming rubble.

I howled in Apple's arms.

Rosie. Rosie.

My other half, who burned, confused and afraid, in a fire I'd caused, who drowned in flame, and, for all she'd flown through the air in her shows, couldn't fly away.

I collapsed back against Apple, rasping silently now instead of crying, my voice worn out, shaking too much even to try to get away anymore. I could hear him murmuring something, and when I looked up, I saw that his eyes were closed in prayer.

In that moment, I knew I was no good to anyone like that — to all the other people's sisters who lay among the circus ruins. All the other people's sisters who might yet be saved.

I forced discipline into my body, something I learned as a

toddling performer long before it was drilled into me as a stage-hand. I forced myself to stand, to make myself ready to help the others.

And then I saw some of the rubble move.

Like a blackened stone pushing up from the earth, a dark bulk rose.

Bear.

Bear, curved around something like he was an arch, a cornerstone, a covered bridge. Curved around something all dark red and gold. Bear, half bald and bleeding with burns, his great, insulating body curved around —

Around Rosie.

Around the small, crumpled blossom of my sister, who still breathed.

ROSIE

Ash.

Loam.

Silence.

Closed
eyes.

Places built
around and under
pain.

Who taught me this trick,
how to leave
the body that hurts?

Who gave me this gift?
We will rest,
she and I.

Until the pain shrinks
into something I can
bear on my back.

Until I can fit
in the costume again,
and bear

to see her
in hers.

We will rest.

IVORY

The circus closed while we made repairs and healed.

Mostly healed.

Even the rebuilding felt like that, like medicine. As if the circus was a sick body that we were nursing back to health.

Except, the body was gone; the main tent had been reduced to ruins. We were rebuilding it from scratch. Reincarnating it.

And I knew the circus's death was all my fault.

The fire. The gas lines. The dallying with Tam that made me triage my way through the preshow checklist.

I might as well have been an arsonist.

In the aftermath, a few members had left, though not more than often did when we arrived in a new city: some of the newer stagehands, a few of the clowns. None of them had been with the circus long enough for me to know them, really. Still, our core remained. Toro took me aside to discuss the financial repercussions of the fire. Vera did what Vera always did: plowed her strength into the cleanup effort and quipped with as much light-heartedness as she could muster. And though it helped with morale, the whole troupe felt like a collective ghost, a spirit, wandering without our body. It was only the main tent that had burned, sure, but that was our heart, our home.

We didn't make campfires at night anymore. Didn't even talk about it — we just abhorred them. We became a cold and quiet group, working silently to bring our body back to life.

I could barely talk, even to Tam. I rested against fer shoulders, as fe did sometimes against mine, and we stroked and braided each other's hair and held each other softly.

But all the kinds of fire, of heat, in me seemed dangerous now — hadn't it been kissing Tam that had kept me distracted from the fire that nearly killed Rosie and Mama?

My father and Rosie's both stayed by Mama's hospital bed day and night, taking it in turns to sleep or to attend to other necessities, which for my father meant his political work, while Rosie's father spent as much time at my sister's bedside as our mother's. When they were both there, each of our fathers held one of Mama's hands.

She wasn't wearing the ring.

The burns were worst on Mama's face, I think because of the beard oil she wore. Her face was bandaged, but we knew the beard was gone. The doctor told us that her skin had been damaged badly enough that probably no hair would ever grow there again.

The old fool said it like it was a blessing, but I knew Mama would mourn the loss when she woke up.

Except she kept not waking up.

I was glad that our fathers were there, because I couldn't be with both Mama and Rosie at the same time. And I was glad that Bear was there to sit with Rosie, because I couldn't be with either her or Mama when I was with the circus. I knew both Mama and Rosie would tell me, if they could, to focus on the circus.

So I tried to be loyal to all three of them. I spent every moment either by their sides or working to restore the circus they both loved.

Lord Bram — my father — paid for the best of everything for Mama and had hired chirurgiennes to see to all the troupe's injuries, even the minor ones. He did that before I'd even had time to think about what would happen to the injured.

He had paid my tuition at Lampton's too. I hadn't known until after I came back, and then only because Vera told me. Mama never did. I'd felt a strange mixture of guilt and thankfulness and anger when I'd learned this — how could I not feel grateful, or guilty, that I hadn't understood to whom I owed my gratitude? Though, of course, Lord Bram had so much money that a year of tuition meant nothing to him.

Would I have stayed at school, I wondered, if I'd known I didn't have to worry about the financial sacrifices I'd thought Mama was making to send me there?

No. I knew that wasn't really why I'd come home. There were other ways I felt indebted to Rosie and Mama and the Circus Rose.

Lord Bram had offered to pay for hospital rooms for everyone, but most of the troupe wanted to stay on the grounds, together, in the tents and caravans they knew. I was sure Rosie would want that too, and I'd argued fiercely to keep her with us.

Her injuries were not superficial; she had a broken arm, and her burns were worse than Mama's. But the Brethren-run hospital's philosophy was all brightness: clean white sheets, mirrors for every gaslight. I could understand it. Everything is spare and clean, and no illness will go unseen.

I knew well, though — better than anybody else — that it was not what Rosie needed. When something bad happens to my sister, what she needs is darkness. Quiet. Solitude, as long as she has me or Bear to share it.

I couldn't watch her flinch and screw up her eyes tight, the way she would when she started to wake up and realized the bright harshness of the environment she was in. It would be like the fire all over again. Even after a good show, Rosie still needed darkness and peace and silence for her mind to heal.

Oh, the doctors could help heal her body — and her body was fit and resilient and would heal the rest of the way on its own.

But her mind needed the quiet that only darkness could give it. That was something the doctors wouldn't understand.

Our fathers didn't understand either . . . but they understood what Bear meant when he stood over her body, silent and hulking, his usually gentle gaze all predator as he simply *dared* someone to try to take her.

And when I snapped at them that I knew what was good for

her better than someone who had never lived in the same home with her a day in her life could ever know, I wounded them both into silence and acceptance. I was glad.

But Lord Bram would hear of nothing but the hospital for Mama, and Mama didn't need the darkness the way Rosie did. So I let him win that point.

The stage crew had some of the worst burns. Apple's hands and forearms were especially bad — I'd seen him pull heavy, flaming benches off several audience members who would have died without his strength and courage. He'd grown quieter than ever; he hated that he'd lost the use of his hands while they healed. He spent most of his time alone, and when I did see him, it was usually with his bandaged arms raised as he knelt in the Brethren manner of prayer.

"May this loss remind us that we never lose what we truly need," I heard him say one night.

He had prayed this way before the fire, but now more of the crew prayed with him. I never joined them.

Three days after the blaze, Ciaran and I were pushing wheelbarrows of sooty rubble toward the fast-growing pile at the edge of the park. Most of the dancing boys had been outside the tent when the fire started, resting and stretching in their long wait until the finale, so they were the least injured of any of us.

They'd done more than their share to step in for the injured crew. The dancing boys were strong, and Ciaran had marshaled them quickly.

"I've always admired the way you lead them," I told him. "It was one of the first things I liked about you."

He glanced at me, a grin lighting up his handsome face. "And here I thought it was my sex appeal!"

I rolled my eyes. "That too."

It was, of course, and we both knew it — just as well as we knew that there was no longer any shred of chemistry or tension between us. That was part of what made Ciaran one of my favorite people to spend time with, even though we were both so busy on our opposite sides of the Circus Rose coin that we rarely had the chance. We'd had a sweet-natured romance that had mellowed out quite naturally into an even sweeter and mellower sense of mutual, platonic support and caring. I knew I could talk to Ciaran about things that were bothering me and he would offer a warm but clear-eyed perspective.

We dumped our wheelbarrows and stood catching our breath for a moment. I pulled my flask from its place at my hip and took a long drink of cool water.

Ciaran reached out for the flask and drank too, then poured a little water on his face and wiped off the soot that streaked his dark brown skin. "I hope you appreciate the sacrifices we're making, Ivory, doing work that messes up our makeup."

"I do." I said it lightly, but as I accepted the flask back from him,

I looked into his eyes. "Truly, Ciaran, I am grateful for everything you and the boys are doing. It's amazing how you've all rallied. You shouldn't have had to do this, none of you. I am sorry you have to."

"Lord, Ivory, what else would we do? Of course we want to help. We're part of this family too."

I didn't quite know what to say to that. The dancing boys were only ever supposed to be with the Rose for a short-term contract. Every time they renewed it, they said that they'd move on when the next renewal came up, but they just loved us too much to leave quite yet — even though they could surely make more money headlining their own show.

Ciaran continued: "And why are you sorry? It's not as if you lit the fire."

I suddenly felt hot, soot-gritty tears start running down my face. "I might as well have. I was negligent. I was supposed to do the safety checks and I rushed through them because — because I was thinking about Tam."

Ciaran knew all about Tam; he was the only person besides Rosie in whom I'd confided about my crush.

He gave me a severe look. "We all rush through things on opening day, Ivory, for goodness sake. It wasn't your fault."

"If I were actually focused on something *worthwhile* instead of just thinking about the next time I'd get to kiss fer — if we hadn't been kissing when the fire started —"

"Ivory. Stop." Ciaran faced me and took both my shoulders in his hands. "I was there when the fire started. I'd slipped back in to watch Rosie's act while my boys were cooling down. It came from nowhere. What on earth could you have done? What could anyone have done but what we did? Do you think I don't wish I was stronger and faster so that I could have gotten more people out more quickly?"

I felt him watching me. "It wasn't your fault," he said, more gently this time. "No more yours than mine or anyone's. It was a horrible accident."

I took a deep breath. "And we're trying to fix it," I said.

He nodded. "Surely that matters more. Besides" — he flashed another of the bright grins I'd once found so irresistible — "what could be more *worthwhile* than kissing?"

We took up the empty wheelbarrows and began the much quicker walk back to the center of the grounds.

Despite Ciaran's good advice, I wasn't quite ready to lose myself in Tam's touch again the way I had when the fire started. But I couldn't stop wanting to spend time with fer.

After an especially long day of managing repairs, I found myself — found, as if I'd been lost — sitting on the ground near the caravan with my head resting on my arms, my eyes closed, feeling as if my body weighed ten thousand times more than I could carry.

I felt someone take my hand and lift it a little, so lightly, and I looked up.

A beautiful freckled face with the darkest and gentlest eyes shining at me — just shining, with a sympathy that didn't hold the slightest trace of pity.

"You deserve to get away for a while," Tam said. "Vera says so too. She'll deal with things for you while we're gone."

I felt tears start to come into my eyes, and Tam hesitated.

"If you'd like, I mean."

I shook the tears away. "I really would."

We walked to a theater a few blocks from the cathedral. It was called the Orpheum, and Mama and Vera had taken Rosie and me to plays there once or twice when we were little. They'd stopped taking us when they realized many of the productions had become morality tales and were sponsored by the Brethren. I'd always thought fondly of the Orpheum, though, and wondered what it would be like to come back.

The air inside was ten degrees cooler, and it smelled like greasepaint. I breathed it in deep. I hadn't been in an audience in so long. Tam walked to the ticket booth and paid for us both before I even had a chance to offer.

"The matinee is just about to start," I heard the woman at the booth say. "You'd better go right in."

And before I knew it, Tam was at my side, taking hold of my arm and pulling me into the theater. "Aisle seats," fe murmured, handing two lilac-colored slips of paper to an indifferent usher. "I couldn't be having you say I'm cheap."

We took our seats at the side aisle of the theater, toward the front, and no sooner had we sat down than the gaslights hissed into nothing and the theater went dark.

"What's the show, anyway?" I whispered, leaning over so I could speak more quietly.

I felt Tam's shrug. "Something from Nordsk, I think," fe said. The curtains opened on a tall, pale woman with a crown in her white hair, wearing a low-cut blue dress. She spoke in Nordsk, a language that sounded mincing and spikily delicate to my ears, and of which I didn't understand a word. Her voice held such urgency, though, that the feeling behind her words was clear. This woman was an excellent actress, that was obvious right away — but behind her, a panel of the background began to move, and words in the common language of Esting appeared on a scroll large enough for the people in the cheapest seats to read.

ARE YOU THERE, MY LOVE? the scroll read.

A man's voice spoke in Nordsk just offstage, and the scroll moved to show, I'M HERE. ONLY COME A LITTLE CLOSER . . .

Already, I was wrapped up in the story on the stage and the clever set design that translated the Nordsk dialogue. *How is it operated?* I wondered.

YOU HAVE GIVEN UP SO MUCH FOR ME, the scroll read as the low voice spoke from offstage. YOUR DUTY, YOUR FAITH, YOUR CROWN —

I WOULD GIVE UP MORE FOR YOUR LOVE, the woman replied, AND FOR OUR CHILD, WHOM I BEAR EVEN NOW.

The woman pulled the crown from her head and tossed it aside. Its points were decorated with Brethren sunbursts; unlike

Esting's royal family, Nordsk's still supported — and were rumored to be largely controlled by — the Brethren.

A flash of gaslight lit the stage with blinding brightness. I was dazzled for a moment, and when my eyes refocused, the woman was cradling a strange thing in her arms, a small writhing black monster. A puppet of some kind, an ugly creature, like a mammalian spider with too much fur and too many legs and teeth.

The woman screamed and tossed the puppet from her, and it flew across the stage. And when it hit the floor, it . . . scuttled. Not like a puppet, but a living creature.

I felt a moment of real horror, even though I knew well it must be only a trained dog in a costume. "A good trick," I whispered to Tam, trying to pretend I was impressed instead of unsettled. But my voice was a little shaky, and fe looked at me with concern.

A black stain appeared on the woman's blue dress, over her belly — a hidden pouch of ink or paint, I thought, still trying not to let it bother me — and she screamed again, clutching at her stomach and breasts, sinking to her knees.

I couldn't say why, but I found myself starting to shake, unable to move from my chair or to stop watching.

I felt Tam's hand cover mine. "Let's go, Ivory," fe said. "This isn't what I was hoping to give you. I'm sorry."

My face felt hot with embarrassment, but I let Tam lead me out of the theater and back into the light of the Port's End afternoon.

ROSIE

The princess shows
me a story. A tale,
like something out of time,

so long ago
it might be yet to come.

It is so near, she says,
but we can see it better
at a distance. So:

So once upon a —
well, you know —

there was a bear.
There was a girl.
There was a man.

He stole the girl's story

and told it himself.

Dearly beloved.

The princess flinches.
The hairs on her arms
prick up, grow thick.

He has a story too, she says.
I know. I'm not trying to say —

The Lord be with you.
The Lord be with your light.
Your love. Your fear.

I'm not trying to say
that he doesn't —

He learned early to call
love and fear
the two sides of one door.

You open
one, and the other

I'm not —

gapes wide.
There are too many
things he learned early.

Not how to fear.
Never that.

Nothing happened to him,
not to him, but he'd seen
enough to know

which side of the lintel
was safe.

He joined the priesthood young.
It is easy to love the Lord.
All-seeing. All-knowing. One.

Humanity is harder.
Messy. Dark. All doors

with doubled sides.
What did they use their will for
but to turn away from God?

He tried, though. Oh, he tried.

They sent him to a snow-capped
parish in the north, and he rose
through its ranks so quickly,
gave clear counsel. What was right

was always clear to him.
He tried to help

them turn from darkness,
truly he did. They just kept
turning back.

They never
feared enough.

He took to walking
through the icy woods.
He came to know the beasts.

Their eyes, all dark,
reflected only light.

Birds darted away. Wolves
slipped between the trees.

A heartbeat: love and fear.

This, *he thought,*
is what we should have been.

He could give them back to God
if only they could see
the world like beasts.

Somewhere under
his voice, the princess
screams, a beastly roar —

A shepherd's flock
is never bred to think.

My story, my story.
Mine mine mine mine mine

We are gathered here today —

He took it from me,
my lover says

under the dream.

I can only claw
it back from him right here.

I need you
to tell me how it ends.

IVORY

The worst thing, every day, was listening to that Brethren preacher Brother Carey — the same priest I'd confronted on opening night. He'd returned with his soapbox and set up at the entrance to the park, telling any passersby who'd listen that the fire was a punishment from the Lord for the circus's many sins.

No — worse than that was how many people listened.

And somehow it was me, Ivory — Ivory, who only ever wanted to be unnoticed and left alone — to whom everyone else looked for leadership. In the absence of Mama, it was me — not Vera or Toro or even Apple — who had inherited the circus and all the responsibilities that entailed.

Most of the time, I wanted to slough off the demands of it all, the way a snake sloughs off a skin that is too tight and itchy and dead, but I knew I couldn't.

It wasn't even that I loved the circus too much to let it die. It was that I loved the ones who loved it, Mama and Rosie, and who were unable to save it themselves.

Everyone kept asking me what we should do, which techniques to use for rebuilding, which suppliers to order from. I would have thought they'd talk to Toro, who kept the accounts, or to Apple. I would never in a million years have thought they'd look to me just because I was Mama's daughter — and I thought Mama herself would balk at such special treatment.

I didn't feel as if I could say any of that to the troupe, though, not even to Ciaran or Tam — things were so fragile, and the healing we were doing was so new. If people wanted to trust me, I couldn't undermine that trust by telling them I doubted myself. I didn't want to risk losing Tam's good opinion — and even Ciaran's sunny faith in me began to feel hollow and tiring.

But there was one person I could talk to, I realized. I'd wanted to avoid him since the day we returned to Port's End, but he was . . . there, all the time. And not part of the circus. And he loved me.

Or so he claimed.

I sat with both our fathers on the sixth day after the fire. I expected I'd have to wait most of the day before Mr. Valko, Rosie's father, would leave Mama's side.

But the redheaded man looked at me sitting across the hospital bed, and then he looked at Lord Bram, nodded, and stood up.

"I'll be back soon, Angela," he told Mama, stroking her wrist carefully, away from the burns. He squeezed my father's shoulder, and my father reached up to grasp his hand. They shared a look full of some feeling I couldn't decipher.

Mr. Valko smiled at me a little sadly. "She's going to pull through, you know," he said. "She always has before."

"I know." I wanted to sound strong, but I'd been holding back tears all day, and the words came out shaky.

He left.

I looked at my father. He looked back at me, and I saw the smile in his eyes before it came to his mouth.

He let go of Mama and reached out his large hands toward mine.

I tried to resist for a moment — then wondered why I was trying. Why, after all, had I come?

I placed my hands in my father's.

They surrounded me, like warm earth around seeds. Like I was returning to some kind of source. I didn't want to like the feeling, but I did.

The tears came then.

Of course.

He held my hands, steady and firm and gentle, while I cried. I hoped fervently that he wouldn't try to embrace me, and he didn't.

He looked at me, and his gaze was steady and gentle too. "What do you need, Ivory?" he asked. "What can I do for you?"

"I need her to wake up," I said. "I don't know how much longer I can manage all of this without her. I don't know how much longer I *should*."

"What has been hardest to manage?" he asked. "Has anyone been mistreating you, been disrespectful? Do you need me to speak to someone?"

"No," I said, hiccupping, "that's just the problem. They've

been *too* respectful. Everyone's assuming I know what to do, how to manage, just because I'm Mama's daughter. They have no idea it's just —" My voice caught. "I don't mean this in a funny way, but it's just . . . it's just an act. I'm just pretending I know what to do."

He regarded me kindly with his dark eyes that were an older version of mine, so different from the light brown eyes Rosie had gotten from Mama. But there was a kind of mourning in his gaze too.

"I suspect the reason they look to you to manage isn't just that you're Mama's daughter. You think logically, make plans, find resources. Just like she always did, in fact. Did you think you'd inherited nothing of her? If it's all an act, it's a convincing one. I, for instance, believe entirely that you're capable of carrying on Angela's work."

I pulled my hands out of his. "But *I* don't believe it. That's the point." I could feel my longing for a father's help curdling back into the anger I'd carried for so long about his absence.

He looked down at his empty hands, and for that moment, I despised him.

"I've never been able to do anything for you, Ivory," he whispered. "I hate myself for it."

I nodded. I kept my face blank and hard, but my sharp rage was already fading away. I wanted so much for him to be . . . I didn't know what. For him to be something to me.

"I should have tried harder to be there for you. I should have fought Angela harder to get to come to your shows, to get to see you. I should have —" He swallowed. "I know I don't deserve to tell you I believe in you. I know I have no right to any part of your life now. But we want to try — Tobias and I both do. We have longed for our daughters, and for Angela, the love of both our lives. In sharing our loneliness, our longing, we've come to love each other too. We hoped that maybe, now that we love each other enough to share our love for Angela, for you two, we might finally get to be together." He looked down at Mama and swallowed, then looked back at me. "I know now that I have no right to you, that I never had a right to your mother. I know that loving someone doesn't mean you own them. But I do believe it means you should try to help them. Please," he said. "Please, let me help you. Tell me how to help you."

Slowly, I told him what the circus needed to keep operating, how he could help me to organize food, clothes, supplies for rebuilding. I wouldn't take more of his money; he'd paid for everyone's care, and I couldn't argue with him about that, but now the circus would mind its own. I'd talked to Toro; we had the funds, just about. It was managing all of it that had me nearly fainting with exhaustion before the morning was even out.

Most of all, I needed Brother Carey to stop his incessant preaching at the gate of Carter Park, in his voice that seemed to wash over us as if amplified by magic, telling everyone who passed by that the fire was a judgment from the Lord and we had deserved far worse than what we got.

It felt like a judgment on me for not double-checking the

gas line. Having my guilt personified in the form of a self-righteous, self-proclaimed holy man was about to break me. I found myself on the edge of tears again just talking about him.

"It's just that shame, on top of everything else," I said, shaking with every word I spoke. "If I didn't feel so ashamed, if there weren't that voice floating through the air making sure I *stayed* ashamed, I think I could bear it."

"Don't worry, darling," my father said. His endearment grated both ways on my heart — he hadn't earned the right to call me *darling*, but I wanted to believe he was going to. "Wait here. We'll sort out everything for you."

I decided to believe him. Right then I needed to believe in someone besides myself.

He left my mother's side, promising me that he and Rosie's father would make sure the Brethren stopped harassing us.

But he never came back.

ROSIE

I keep
waking up
alone.

Where is she?
Where is she?

I push myself back
into sleep,
a muzzy shroud
plush as a thousand
furs, a place at least
as dark and soft
as her.

A spotlight searches.

A place I can
pretend.

An empty stage.

In sleep I am
never
alone.

Is she here?

Burial in dream
is better; after all,
I've only really
touched her there.

Won't meet
the light alone.

Better the dark
than that
bright loneliness
of waking
where things are only
what they seem to be.

Where is she?

IVORY

The next day, my father's valet appeared at the gate to Carter Park. A tall, fat man in an impeccably tailored indigo coat with gold trim, he radiated the wealth and status that he represented on Lord Bram's behalf. He gave Brother Carey and his soapbox a dignified sneer as he marched up to the circus grounds and asked me, in the most discreet and roundabout manner possible, if Lord Bram had spent the night there.

"He seems to be missing, miss," he said, his formal tone barely hiding his genuine fear.

I despised myself for it a little, but I was relieved; there was a reason my father hadn't given me the help he promised.

I despised myself more for my next thought — that even if he'd died, for a moment, I'd still had a good father.

The police arrived only a few hours after the valet left. The troupe was getting ready for dinner, but I hadn't managed to work up an appetite to join them. I kept pacing, watching the gate as if it were the site of an open wound, where infection might seep in.

The first thing I noticed about them were the silver buttons on their gray uniforms glittering in the setting sun. They each gave a friendly nod to Carey as they passed him. I shouldn't have been surprised that they approached me first, not when I was standing there staring at them like a sentry, but I still wasn't used to being read as a leader.

"We're here to look into the whereabouts of Lord Bram," the shorter of the two officers said sternly. Even as she spoke, the other officer was sweeping past us onto the grounds. "Can you account for your activities last night?"

I flinched. "What do you mean?"

The officer looked me up and down. "You were one of the last to see him. We're going to need to search these premises to see if there's anything suspicious here." She glanced behind me, one eyebrow raised, as if the very fact of who we were was already suspicious enough.

The headache that had been lurking at the back of my skull over the long workday crackled into real pain. I had to close my eyes for a moment, and when I opened them again, the officer was frowning at me. "Well?"

"Excuse me," I heard a soft voice say from behind me, "do you have a warrant?"

The sound of fer voice made the pain in my head lessen just enough that I could look the officer in the eye again. "Do you?" I echoed Tam.

"Carter Park is a public space," she said tersely. "We don't need a warrant."

"But the tents and caravans are our homes," I said. "Those are private."

Tam had come to stand beside me, shoulder to shoulder. Fe nodded. "We're concerned about Lord Bram ourselves," fe said. "He's been an immense help in the wake of the fire."

The officer's eyes narrowed. "Yes, been giving you and yours a lot of his resources, hasn't he?" she said. But when neither of us responded, she sighed. "Right. Goring!" she called, and the other officer was back at her side quicker than I would have thought possible.

Tam and I kept standing together until they were well out of the park; until they had vanished down the road.

"I should have thought to ask them for a warrant right away," I said. "I don't know how many times we'd be in some city and something would happen, a theft or an attack, and the circus was the first place people looked for those who were guilty. No one likes to think the danger comes from their own, not with someone else around to blame." I looked over at fer. "How did you . . ."

"You should have seen the police force Esting had in Faerie when it was occupied," fe said. "You have to know how it works, and sometimes even then . . ." Fe shook fer head. "These two were nothing."

Tam's expression was still neutral, still gentle, but something in fer eyes had gone hard.

I reached out, and as lightly as I could, I touched fer shoulder.

I'd thought at first that my father just hadn't kept his promise.

That in itself had been no surprise.

At least, I'd kept reminding myself that I shouldn't be surprised.

But I had *wanted* my father to leap in and save the day, even though I knew that was such a foolish, predictable wish that it verged on boring.

"I should have been too smart for this," I told Tam, who had been sitting in shared silence with me for a long while after the dinner I couldn't make myself eat, watching the stars appear in the evening sky as the sunset slipped away.

Fe twined fer fingers through mine. "Too smart for what?"

"I shouldn't have let myself believe my father could help. What has he ever, ever done to make me think I could?"

"Oh, Ivory," Tam said. "It doesn't make you foolish to hope, to trust someone. It makes you good." Fe brought our heads close together, and I felt fer eyelashes flutter briefly against my forehead.

The contact felt good, grounding, and I leaned into it. "I still don't see why you like me so much, Tam," I said. "You're so . . . you're magic, and *gorgeous*, and I'm . . . a backstage girl. Not that I'm not happy about all this, but . . ."

Tam didn't say anything to that; fe just looked at me, but fe looked in a warm, steady way that grew slowly darker, deeper, more quietly admiring, and that told me, if not *why* fe liked me, at least that fe absolutely did.

And for the first time since the fire, when I felt the answering warmth blossoming through my body, I didn't push it away. I reached up and stroked Tam's hair, tucking a curl behind fer slightly pointed ear.

Our faces were still so close together that it only took the smallest movement, after that, to bring my lips to meet fers.

I shivered as fe returned my kiss, shivered with how much I'd missed just this kind of warmth.

The sweetness of Tam's breath mingled with mine, and fer soft mouth was like a healer's touch. I closed my eyes and became, for a moment, only a kiss.

When warmth had filled every corner of my body, I touched fer face again and pulled away.

"That's the first time we've kissed since the fire, you know," I said. Part of me felt it was time to stop talking, wanted to lose my thoughts inside Tam's kisses again, now that I felt I could. But my thoughts were less painful when I could talk them through with fer. They turned bearable, and sometimes, even sweet.

"I know," fe said. "I figured you'd let me know when you were ready."

"Yes." I laughed a little.

We took long, matching breaths. It was something Rosie and I used to catch ourselves doing accidentally — matching our breaths to each other. In the caravan with Bear, she wasn't far away . . . and yet she was, and I missed her.

"Oh, Ivory," Tam said suddenly, "trusting your father, whether he deserves it or not . . . it makes you *brave*. Where would I be if I hadn't trusted your mother and joined the Rose and come here, to a country that has been cruel to mine over and over? I'd be nowhere I want to be. I'd be nowhere near you."

"I'm not as brave as *that*, Tam. Setting off from Faerie with us, it seems amazing to me. Leaving the only life you'd ever known . . ."

"Like you did when you left the circus for engineering school? Was it foolish to chase a dream then, to have a little faith? And is it any less foolish, really, to hope your father was becoming the kind of parent he always should have been? If there's stupidity there, Ivory, or fault, it's his. When someone hurts you, it's their fault, not yours for letting them." Fe took my face in fer hands and kissed me gently . . . and then not so gently. "Ivory, you are so, so brave."

About then, I became very aware of the presence of other troupe members nearby, and I led Tam away to a quiet edge of the park that the fire had never reached.

ROSIE

Is this
what it is

for her:
the body

a painful
stranger?

I won't go back
without her.

I dream
the princess,
here.

Her long
pale hair,
like snow,

like stars.
Her eyes
like ice.

A delicate touch,
a softness,
in her

lips.

Oh, my
princess,
snow-night girl,
never feeling
but through
fur,

the body her
rightful inheritance
trapped in
the bear they call
him.

I dream of her.
I hold her, there,
in dream, the body

that hides
in her
heart.

I know
she dreams of me.

I see her.
I can *see*.

IVORY

Vera and Toro and Apple took turns with me by Mama's side, now that Rosie's and my fathers were gone.

They'd vanished completely. Not a strange thing, perhaps, for Tobias Valko, a sailor from Nordsk who seemed to have known practically no one in Port's End save my parents, but Lord Bram was an active presence in the city. There were plenty of people who wondered where he had gone.

No one had any idea.

It was strange how easy it was just to pretend I'd never seen him at all. Never felt that wild seasick rush of mingled resentment and hope when I saw the ring he and Mr. Valko gave Mama. Never woken up the dreams I used to cherish when I was a little girl. They were still there somewhere, hiding in the back of my mind, behind a wall of light I made so bright I couldn't see past it.

After a while, there were almost as many missing posters for Lord Bram papering the city as Brethren propaganda.

I tried to ignore them both. All I let myself care about was the circus and when Mama and Rosie would get well.

The doctors said Mama was healing, and her sleep, in the meantime, was easy. She always had one of us with her too.

I poured myself into healing the circus, directing and delegating and doing all the things that I'd whispered to my father were just an act.

At least, I thought, as I helped mark places for new tent posts one afternoon, I had people to delegate to. Five footmen and three housemaids from my father's estate arrived on Monday morning and quickly fell to whatever task I asked them to do. Vera and Toro too. The more leadership roles I took over, though, the less pretense it became, and when my work was mostly done each evening and I was too tired to do more, there was the lovely sweetness of Tam's arms to melt into, the joy I found in fer words and touch and kisses.

It felt like fe needed that just as much as I did, and it was good to feel needed, longed for, when fe was asking for the same thing I wanted to give. The circus needed so much from me, things I found exhausting sometimes — things I did out of the kind of love that could just as easily be called obligation. What I did with Tam was . . . celebration. I couldn't get enough.

And still, fe started saying that one day fe would leave.

It was the Brethren who were driving Tam away, I thought. Brother Carey and his soapbox. The flyers everywhere. The dirty looks fe got, that all the Fey got, all over Port's End.

The war is over, I wanted to say to my fellow Estingers, *and the Fey didn't start it to begin with.*

But I knew I couldn't make it right, couldn't even protect Tam from the way people called magic "tricks" or "curses," from the hostility that could suddenly fill the air when someone saw that fe was Fey.

A child of about ten came up to Tam while we were walking down the street one afternoon. "I saw you at the pier that day," she said shyly. "You were my favorite."

Tam smiled and leaned down to talk to her. "Thank you so much. Performing magic is my favorite thing."

"My dad liked you too. He wanted to know . . ." She blushed.

My hackles rose, but Tam's face stayed serene. "To know what, darling?"

"Do you think you'd be a man or a woman, if you were a person?"

Just the smallest flinch from Tam, but that kind smile stayed on fer face. A true performer. "I am a person, just as I am. You can tell your father that." Fe took a deep breath, straightening again. "Here." Fer left hand moved in a small circle, and a sphere of purple light grew before the child's face. It shimmered and broke apart, revealing a white bird inside.

Tam gestured again, and the lights vanished. The girl blinked in wonder, her father's question forgotten.

"If I didn't like you so much, I think I'd be gone already," fe told me as we walked away. Once we were alone again, the anger in fer usually calm voice was palpable. "I thought it would be . . . The war is over. We're supposed to be free."

"You are," I said. "I'm — I'm sorry that happened. I'm sorry things like that keep happening. But Esting will get better. Give them time. Give us time."

Fe shook fer head. "I'm always a person in Faerie."

We tore down a few more Brethren flyers as we walked through the city.

HELLFIRE COMES EARLY TO SINNERS one said.

LET GOD'S LIGHT IN BEFORE IT BURNS YOU read another.

I was shaking by the time we got back to Carter Park and the picketers at the gate.

"Ignore them," Tam murmured. "I've seen far worse."

Fe wrapped an arm around my waist, and I did the same to fer. I knew I had far less right to feel scared of the picket line than fe did.

As we passed through the protesters, Tam stared down several of them, most of whom glanced away after a mere second or two; I wasn't strong enough for that. I just kept looking at the still-hollow center of the circus grounds, where our huge, frilled tent had stood. Where Mama ought to be setting up for the night's show. And the row of caravans and dressing tents, now half given over to makeshift sickbeds for the wounded.

When Tam and I finally had another moment together at the end of that long day, drinking tea under the cloudy night sky, I knew that fer heart was as heavy as mine. Fer dreams of what traveling the world would be like had fallen apart, and I . . . I couldn't pretend I hadn't started to have a few dreams of my own about what a future away from the circus might look like, a future that I could love. In one of those bookshelf-street townhouses, with ivy on the walls to show how long they'd stood in the same place. With a steady job that would keep my feet on the ground. And just maybe with someone like Tam — quiet and steady and lovely. We could be there for each other, always there, when we came home.

The first step down that road was still Lampton's. I had missed Mama and Rosie so much when I was there that I'd had to come back to the circus, but I found I missed the school nearly as much now. Was that what happened to anyone who loved two places: their heart was always torn in half?

I thought of Mama's ring, secreted away in the caravan. And I wondered if, maybe, I was starting to understand why she'd refused to choose between our fathers, even if that choice left Rosie and me without either of them.

I hadn't known to be grateful, growing up, that my whole heart had lived in one place. Now some small part of me lived always inside of Tam, and some larger part — a dream I still couldn't let go of — was at engineering school . . .

But I knew my only dream should be that Rosie and Mama would get better. And part of me still wondered whether the fire had been my fault; whether I had almost caused —

I could barely even think it.

I knew neither Rosie nor Mama would believe my negligence had caused the circus fire, so I tried not to believe it either.

Slowly, I began to succeed — at leading, at believing. At everything.

And then Rosie woke up.

8

ROSIE

I
know
that
voice.

IVORY

I was going over the work schedule with Apple and Toro — enough of the crew were still nursing their wounds that everyone who could was working triple shifts, and no one was happy about it, either — when suddenly I heard a voice that I had never heard before.

"Rosie," it was saying, soft and low. "Rosie, Rosie." A voice as gentle, as tactile as the wind through my hair.

I didn't bother to look up at Toro or Apple, didn't bother to find out if they'd heard it too. I just turned and followed the voice I didn't recognize as if I never knew how to do anything else.

It was coming from the caravan where Rosie slept. I don't know how I didn't think, didn't realize, as I moved toward it, but I didn't . . .

Inside, in the darkness that Rosie needed, I couldn't see anything for a moment.

Then, as shapes began to resolve themselves, at first I saw only one great circle, red, dark, breathing. That low voice came from the darkness, and so did a small yawning breath that I knew well. Rosie waking up.

The whites of two human eyes flashed toward me.

The redder part of the darkness became my sister, and the darker, Bear.

I rushed forward and pulled Rosie to me, forgetting her injuries, forgetting everything.

My sister put her half-healed arms around me.

This body I held was one mine had known before I was born. My limbs had been so lonely for my sister.

I shuddered and held her tight.

But as soon as I lifted her off of Bear, she started to cry — small wheezing, mewling cries like a newborn baby. Her hands reached out toward Bear, and her cries escalated toward something that would have been screaming if she'd had more strength.

"We're here, Rosie, we're right here! You're all right!" I said. My eyes had accepted the dark now, and I could see the places where her skin was still raw, where the salt in her tears must have stung as it tracked down her face.

She cried louder. A scab on her cheek split and wept.

Bear pressed his nose on Rosie's face again.

But that did not stop her crying out, either.

"Rosie," that incomprehensibly gentle and deep voice muttered. Bear pressed his muzzle more firmly to my sister's face. "Rosie."

The voice was coming from Bear.

The voice was Bear's.

My mouth went dry as air. I tried to swallow but could not.

"Bear?"

Bear looked at me with eyes as dark and deep as forests, his nose still pressed to Rosie's brow.

"Oh, Princess," Rosie breathed, finally seeming to settle, to come back into herself. "You're still here."

I stared.

ROSIE

Ivory thinks
I am the one
who needs.

Bear loves her too.
Loves her too much
to lie, except
by silence.
Enough to know
how best to love.

How could she take
away a third father?

IVORY

I couldn't move.

How could I not have known? How could I not have been told?

How could Bear not have wanted to talk to me?

I'd felt so guilty, leaving Rosie to go to Lampton's. I thought I'd broken the most profound promise I'd ever made: to never leave her alone.

And all along, there was a place in her life, in her heart, that was completely separate from me. Even from Mama.

There was something in our home that was not as it seemed. And it made Rosie not quite what she'd seemed either; it made me wonder if she needed me less than I thought she did.

If I'd known she didn't need me, maybe I would have stayed at school . . .

I couldn't finish that thought. It hurt too much.

Bear blinked at me slowly. Lying next to him, still weak, Rosie looked at me too and nodded.

Why won't you talk now? I thought at both of them.

But as much as I despised them for keeping Bear's voice a

secret, just then, the weight of that pain was outbalanced by my relief that Rosie was finally awake again.

"Ivory," Bear rumbled. "Ivory . . ."

Something in Bear's deep, strange, animal voice reminded me too much of my father saying *darling*, and suddenly I wanted to scream.

"Stop it," I said, and even I could hear how harsh my voice was. "You never bothered to talk to me before, so I don't want to hear you now. Just be" — my father's hand in Rosie's father's, in Mama's, in mine — "just be Bear."

Bear rumbled again, but it was a wordless noise, a Bear noise. He lowered his great head to look in my eyes.

His eyes were still talking, of course. The sweet, dark, calm eyes of the beast who had looked after me since I was seven. They were saying . . .

"She loves you," Rosie said. "She loves you so much, you know."

"Who, the *princess?*" I started to shake. "Rosie, how is it possible for you and I to be so different? I've never understood — I can't —" The shaking was getting so bad that it threatened to knock me down. I couldn't even remember why I'd wanted to talk to her in the first place, this sister whose mind followed such different lines from my own. Even my twin, the person I loved most in the whole world, was someone I could love but could not know.

"I'm sick of this. All this smoke and mirrors. And then the fire, and you and Mama gone, and I've been running everything, and our fathers gone, and everyone looking to me — I've had to make so many decisions, I don't know how there's even enough of me left to talk to you with right now — and Bear said our names, and you woke up —"

Bear had moved toward me while I spoke, and I was still shaking, but his huge warm bulk was there against me, and my body leaned into it without my meaning to. Rosie's still-bandaged hand reached out and touched my hair.

I had never understood my sister. We loved each other, we protected each other and helped each other survive in all the strangeness that had surrounded us as we grew up, but there was some profound gulf of difference between us that we rarely crossed. We were twins, but our minds, our hearts, followed such different rhythms that if we'd met as strangers, I'd often thought, we likely wouldn't have been friends.

But something in us, sometimes, bridged the gap.

ROSIE

"Tell me," she says.
"Just tell me why
I never knew before."

How to say it?
How to heal this?

"Would you give
away the Bear
you grew up with
all of these years?"

Ivory shivers again.
My hand and Bear's
breath steady her.

"No. I couldn't have.
But now I do.
I want to know. Bear,

tell me. Please.
Tell me who
you really are."

A rumble in
my sweetheart's chest.
The girl I've never touched
now speaks.

IVORY

"She's only ever spoken to me," Rosie said quietly. "And you, now." Her voice quavered a little with something that sounded almost like jealousy.

I swallowed painfully.

"Bear loves us. And Mama. And all the family. That much is true. That much is real."

They both nodded, my sister's head and Bear's moving in a strange kind of synchrony, for all they were so mismatched in size.

We are what's real, I thought, Mama's voice in my head as if she stood by my side.

I was crying, but it didn't matter.

"Right," I said. "Tam and I need to sort out dinner. Bear . . ." The plans formed themselves only as I spoke them aloud. I didn't know how to fix any of this, how to make anything be what it was supposed to be again—the circus, Bear, Mama—but I would deal with what was in front of us. It was all I could do.

I couldn't speak for another moment, remembering Bear's voice. We looked at each other.

"Can you say anything else?" I asked at last.

Bear gazed at me for a long time. Finally he opened his mouth wide, showing white teeth the size of my fingers, and roared.

Then he closed his mouth calmly and dipped his head, giving me a little circus bow.

Bear was still Bear.

Bear laid his snout along my shoulder and whuffled. Just like a bear.

I leaned my head against his, and he was only what he'd ever been.

Then I went out to face what needed facing.

ROSIE

I dreamed a memory.

Mama gathering
us up from the campfire side
after one too many
questions about our fathers.

"Who needs a father when
they have Bear, and all of you,
and me?" In a voice
that tried so hard
to prove she believed
she was enough for us.

I could always hear that lie,
bravado like bearskin
bristling, covering the unseen
girl inside, some part of Mama
who always feared

she couldn't give back to us
what she'd taken away
when she left our fathers.

I often wondered,
in a very Ivory way,
if Mama only thought
she'd have one fatherless girl
no matter what —
and it wouldn't be right,
be fair, to let one of us have
what the other might always want.

What I knew, of course,
is that there had always been
a right choice. Ivory
missed a father more
than I ever had or ever
thought I could.

I only feared
how easy it would be
for them to take Mama away from us,
if she could ever
have them both.

IVORY

"How are we supposed to go on without our tent?" I asked Tam in frustration over burnt porridge I'd attempted to make in the huge black cauldron. "How are we supposed to have any show at all? A tent and a ring are what make a circus!"

Tam looked at me shrewdly. "I could magic something to look a little like a ring. It'd just be a loop of light, but it might do . . . and you're an engineer, aren't you, Ivory?"

"I'm not an engineer. I've had one year of engineering school," I said. "If you study something for one year, all you find out is how many things you don't know. The girls who've been there five years or more could maybe come up with something, working together. And the teachers, of course. Not me."

And then I knew.

I leapt up like a mad scientist, like I had showmanship in me after all. I smiled at Tam. "The circus is saved!" I cried.

Fe leapt up too, applauding. "Brava!"

9

IVORY

Thanks to the aerograms that Miss Lampton herself had invented, my plea for help arrived at the Lampton School in far-away Woodshire not even two hours after I sent it, and I had my old headmistress's reply shortly after lunch (which I also burned).

My students are delighted to receive such an intriguing assignment, she wrote. *I hadn't even finished reading your message out loud before Dimity started making diagrams. I and five of the girls will arrive tomorrow, supplies in hand, and the rest of the students at Lampton all beg to be remembered to you — too many to name here, although I'm sure you remember them equally well as they do you. You'll be pleased to reunite with the girls I'm bringing, I know. Thank you, Ivory, for the chance to give my students such a useful and fascinating bit of real-world application. I have no doubt this will be the most fun we'll have all year, and we're all grateful to you already.*

Well, I was grateful to her for saying she was grateful, anyway. It made her coming so quickly feel less like pity.

The Lampton School's airship, the *Spirit of Jules*, was comically small compared to the ones the circus hired for traveling; it was more like a private lake boat than a cruise ship or carrier vessel. Not much larger than a carriage, really, if you didn't count the balloon that kept it airborne. I wasn't sure how its six passengers could even fit inside along with the supplies Miss Lampton had mentioned in her letter when I saw it in the sky at breakfast the following day. That meal, at least, had not been burned thanks to Tam's insistence that fe take over cooking duties.

That was probably just more pity, but I was as ready as anyone to eat a meal that didn't taste quite so strongly of char, so I conceded without a fight. As the *Spirit of Jules* approached and descended onto the flame-scarred field, I saw how they fit; everyone had stayed on the above decks for the whole journey, strapped securely into light-framed chairs around the perimeter. They all wore caps and goggles, and every one of them clutched the identical lidded teacups I'd grown very familiar with on picnic excursions during my year at school.

Miss Lampton herself stood at the prow of the airship, the top of her head nearly brushing the light blue balloon, a color that blended with the cloudless morning sky. She expertly brought the ship to hover about ten feet above the ground, and I held out my hands to catch the rope that one of the students — I couldn't recognize her yet, what with the goggles — threw to me. I tied it to one of the tent stakes, thinking with not a little sourness that at least now the stake had some kind of use, and on the other side of the ship, a rope ladder unfurled to the ground.

Miss Lampton cut the engine, and I could suddenly hear the babble of the girls' talk filling the air. My heartbeat sped up. It was almost as if I were back at school again.

They tumbled out of the airship, scrambling down the ladder and across the singed and trampled grass, until I was tackled in the center of five hugs at once. "Oh, Ivory, we've missed you!" Dimity cried. "I've missed you! How dare you wait this long to invite us to your circus!"

Behind the throng of girls, I glimpsed Miss Lampton grinning at us as she shielded her eyes from the sun, looking around the field. Her expression told me she was the gladdest of anyone to see me again—and it somehow seemed as if she were even proud. I thought that must have been just residual pride in her other students. After all, what could I show her now that would do her credit? All my projects had been lost in the fire. I hadn't found even traces of them in the rubble.

But it was useless to think of any of that now. I hugged as many of the girls as I could reach. "Dimity, Rachida, Constance, Felicity, Faith!" I laughed. "I can't believe I get to see all of you again!"

When they'd finally unhanded me, I waved Tam over to the circle and made introductions. They all seemed fairly awestruck by fer beauty—as who would not be?—and I felt a kind of possessive pride in fer. I had to keep myself from preening outright when fe took my hand as we led the girls and Miss Lampton to ground zero of the tent's destruction.

"Well," she said, "this will be quite a project."

ROSIE

Ivory talked about them. All
those girls,
in her letters from school. Friends, rivals,
roommates.

Living packed
close together
as queen cakes
in a pastry tin.

I couldn't have borne it.
We were the only
girls our age
the circus ever had.

Between Ives and Mama
and the family, and
always, thank goodness,
Bear, I was never alone.

But I never knew, either,
what I had missed.
All those girls,
all around me?
I'd have burst.

Exploded.
Dissolved.
Absolutely
swooned.

Even watching
them now, from the caravan
shadows, sends my
skin burning again.

Their casual, careening embraces.
Their kisses on
my sister's cheek
arrive like cool ghosts
to my own.

Bear rumbles, in darker
shadows. "Are you jealous,
my darling?" I ask.
No words in reply.

No words ever,
but my name
and Ivory's.
That much is true.
I know, as Ivory
doesn't, the years
Bear worked to shape
her animal throat
to the sound of two
names she loves.

I leave the window,
settle my skin
into resting again.
As I settle

the rest of me down,
my hand on Bear's paw,
to dream of the
princess again,

the light still falls
through the pane and
fills
the bed.

IVORY

The girls soon had the circus well in hand. I could hardly believe the amount of supplies they'd stored away in that little toy airship of theirs, and Miss Lampton insisted that they were all covered by class expenses. We'd had costlier projects when I was a student, not least among them creating a pair of wind-up ballet dancers to perform for the Royal Exhibition of Art and Science, so I didn't argue — not that I had the budget to argue in earnest, anyway.

Skeletons of new tents were erected by the end of the following day; Dimity's blueprints had made it clear that it would be much easier to create three small interconnected tents than try to build a single huge one in a matter of days. Tam's "loops of light" inside the tents meant we didn't even need footlights; the rings would be moodily lit and silver-dim, but I actually liked that better. "More shadows means more room for roughness in the props and sets," I said.

"Spoken like a true stagehand," Tam replied, molding the line of light along the ground like clay in fer hands.

Between the engineering students and the remaining stage-hands and troupe — working in shifts, granted, all hours of the day and night — we skimmed along toward Saturday morning in a blur, since I hoped reopening that weekend would begin to get the circus back on its financial feet, something I wanted to happen as soon as possible. On Friday night, we went back to selling tickets.

Of course, Brother Carey was still there warning people away. I tried to remember Mama's insistence that he was the best advertising we could get . . . but the fire had been the worst. Even a child could make the connection between his preaching about brimstone and divine punishment and the inferno in the tent.

He talked about hellfire and holy light and the Lord's bright glare so often, though, that I began to have my own ideas about what — or who — might have started the fire. And it wasn't the Lord, in whom I still didn't put much stock.

But just as I had pointed out to Brother Carey that the circus had the right to make use of public spaces, so too did he. So I settled for staring daggers into his back whenever my chores and errands forced me to walk by him at the park's entrance — not more than two or three times a day, thank goodness. His unsettling, pale gaze was bad enough when it only came as often as a meal.

And so we found ourselves opening again on Saturday night, a new kind of circus, smaller but still coming back fighting.

I watched everyone get set up, overseeing what I could. Vera was going to be mistress of ceremonies — that was one job I knew for sure I couldn't handle, even though she had pointed out multiple times that I was the one who had earned the title these last weeks, who had been mistress of the circus, who had kept everything going, who had called in the Lampton girls to help us rebuild.

Miss Lampton found me before the show started and gave me a hug. "The Circus Rose is a bouquet now," she said, looking at the low, triple-crowned tent she and her students had designed.

I gave a startled laugh. "Maybe it always should have been," I said. And then, "Thank you so much."

Miss Lampton squeezed my shoulder again. "I'm going to get a sinnum bun and watch the show with my girls," she said, "something I've been waiting to do since I first met you, Ivory. I'll come congratulate you after the show." She winked at me and was off.

I spent the whole show pacing the three tents, tracing the perimeters of Tam's lights. I knew well that they couldn't catch fire — fe'd assured me of that countless times, and the bluish-pink light even felt cool, not warm, when I passed my hand through it. But still I worried.

Another fire would annihilate us completely.

ROSIE

How strange to watch
the show backstage.
Too injured now.
Too raw. Too new.
And sister too afraid
to see me freeze
or burn again —
I know she
could not stand
to see me fly.

But it is dark
back here.
Darkness is good.
Is blessed. It lets
me rest. Until she heals
Bear has no act either.
I rest against
her side, her paw

curled back into my lap,
heavy as a sleeping child.

How magical, this gift.
To watch, to wait.
My heart is impatient
to leap again,
but it has been so long
since I have seen,
from the sweet outside,
this bright glow.

IVORY

Tam couldn't perform and control the lights at the same time, so we'd lost another of our top acts even though fe was still right here with us. Fer lights were a definite hit, however — although magic hadn't been illegal since King Finnian was crowned, it was still controversial enough that most people stuck to Estinger tech.

I was selfishly gleeful that fe'd defected to the stagehand side. And in my pacing, I got to pass by fer several times, sitting tailor-style in the shadows at the edge of the third ring, breathing as slowly as if in meditation but with fer eyes wide open.

I didn't dare kiss fer or anything so intimate, not wanting to disturb fer too much, but fe smiled up at me every time I passed, and I smiled back and brushed fer cheek with the back of my hand or ran my fingers lightly through fer hair. Every touch was grounding, quieting the edge of panic that kept lancing through me, as if my fears were lightning and Tam were a strong tree, connected to the damp ground, that could take my energy down and dissipate it in the infinite earth.

Finally the show was over: bows, applause, and even an

encore. Just one, but it was enough to allay my fears for at least a little while.

"Thank you, everyone!" cried Vera. "Please tell your friends — there are more wonders waiting for you here tomorrow night in the first-ever three-ring circus!"

When the final chords of the finale faded away, I felt my whole body shudder with relief. The show had ended, and nothing had burned, and everyone was safe. As I watched the smiling, murmuring audience pour out of the three connected tents, I let myself think that it had even been a success.

Tam stood up, still breathing deeply and evenly, although I could see a light sheen of sweat on fer brow. "A three-ring circus," fe said, coming over to put fer arm around me. "Isn't there something about that that just sounds right?"

I smiled. "You're done working," I said.

Fe looked at me, nonplussed. "I am . . ."

"Then I can distract you." I slipped my arms around Tam's neck and kissed fer soundly, and for a few moments, I forgot everything but how we felt together.

Then we went to find Rosie and Bear.

As we neared the spot backstage from which my sister had watched the show, I began to shake with relief, and I felt tears starting in my too-dry, tired eyes.

Now, at last, I could believe that we were going to make things work, that the Circus Rose would still be here for Mama when she woke up.

"There'll be a circus for Mama to come home to," I said when I finally sat down next to Rosie. "That's what matters. We have to keep it going."

"The show must go on," she murmured.

As the last of the crowds drifted away from the park, the troupe finally gathered for our midnight supper.

I stood by the fire, ready to hand out portions to everyone; I didn't feel I could breathe until I'd congratulated all of the performers and crew.

With my fears unrealized, I became aware anew of my huge gratitude for my former teacher and classmates. I'd seen them in the audience, and they'd been thrilled, but I hadn't seen them since. I thought Miss Lampton might have taken them off to a late supper in the city — or that they might already be asleep. They deserved a rest maybe more than any of us.

Except — hadn't Miss Lampton said she'd come congratulate me after the show?

My heart banged up into my throat, and I left the fireside and walked quickly, then half ran, toward the *Spirit of Jules* and the tent the girls had pitched underneath it.

No one was there.

I ran back toward the campfire, and Apple met me on the border of its light.

"Ivory, none of us can find Vera, Bonnie, or Toro. I think you need to come see this."

He showed me the area backstage where they had been bantering and cleaning off their makeup just a little while before. Rosie, Bear, and Tam huddled together there, looking at the ground, where drops of blood soaked into the grass.

ROSIE

Ivory's magic lover
raises the alarm.

I climb on Bear,
my princess,

for her
warmth and my comfort

and we follow.
We find the scene

where Vera
last was seen.

Scattered ribbons,
spilled rouge,

a tidy box of stockings,

all knocked over —

no choice to leave,
not her choice. Blood

on the ground,
dark like dirt.

Bear smells it,
points it out,

metal tang rising
over the scent of the crowd.

Not enough
for us to notice,

our sad human
senses. Not enough

to mean that Vera
won't have lived.

Enough to know
she didn't want to go.

IVORY

"I was just here," Tam whispered. "I was just with them . . ."

"Did you hear anything?" I asked Apple.

"Nothing." The lashes under his eyes were wet. "Nothing."

None of us could stop looking down at the small drops of blood on the ground that Bear had found.

"Vera's blood?" I asked. "You're sure?"

I realized that most of the troupe was now gathered around Bonnie's dressing table. All of them were watching me. Not looking at the scene of Bonnie's usually neat toilette all overturned, nor Vera's dumbbells on the ground spattered with blood and — now, that was odd — some kind of white hair.

All of them were watching me.

And all my aching muscles felt so weak, and my throat caught, and my eyes grew once again too dry.

And I couldn't stand any of it anymore.

I needed my mama.

ROSIE

Through the gate
of Carter Park
and past
the picket line.
The Brother who burned
so terribly bright is gone.

Ivory and I walked
alone.
I longed to hide
my face in Bear's thick fur.

I held my head
up high and kept it clear,
staring straight
ahead and into nothing,
praying my mind
wouldn't let too much in.

Ivory watched it all.
She looked them in the eye.
She never had to learn,
as I did,
how to keep her thoughts
from screaming.
I felt her heart
break all the way there.

To the hospital,
so white it hurt
to look at, even
at night.

A sister nurse
watched as we passed
the atrium, and Ivory
nodded to say she knew her.
It was nighttime. We met
no one else.

Most people fear the dark, but
what's scarier than an empty spotlight
after the performer's cue?
Bright — bright and searingly empty.

The bed barely disturbed — she couldn't
put up a fight — empty and white as
a blank eye, no blood, the only red
Mama's ringmistress jacket,
still neatly folded over a chair.

Ivory and I alone
in this burning silence.

Ivory tears at the bedding,
like this is another mystery she can solve
by pulling things apart.

Aha!
She holds up a swath of gauze
fallen off Mama's arm as they took her.

IVORY

Beside me at Mama's empty bed, Rosie was doubled over, holding the scrap of gauze that had bound Mama's wounds.

"Oh, Rosie, I'm sorry," I whispered. "I'm so sorry."

"Sorry?" Her voice was a rasp.

I flinched. "If I'd just checked the gaskets, I had time, I was so stupid —"

"Ivory." Her voice was shaky. "No. The fire wasn't your fault. Don't you hear what they're saying outside the circus? All that shouting about hellfire?"

ROSIE

What is the opposite
of a mystery?

IVORY

I asked the first nurse I found if she knew what happened to our mother. The question caused a flurry of activity — it was very clear no one had expected an unconscious patient to disappear — but neither Rosie nor I had any hope they would find her. We walked back to the circus, passing so many Brethren posters along the way, as Rosie made a convincing case that they were the ones behind both the fire and the disappearances.

Back at Carter Park, I held the gauze beneath Bear's nose. He huffed over it, separating Mama's scent and the tang of hospital disinfectant from the one who took her.

"And you're sure it's Brother Carey?"

Rosie glared at me. "You're meant to be the logical one, Ivory. Can't you put the pieces together?"

Bear watched me too, his expression as fierce as my sister's. In all the years he had played the beast in our circus, I had never seen even a hint of real anger, of anything frightening or even *wild* in his demeanor. But now Bear growled, rage like a fire behind his eyes.

I could see that pain, that rage. I knew it, because I shared it.

I didn't know who else would vanish, but I was sure now, beyond any shadow of a doubt, that they had been taken.

They'd been taken.

Rosie was right. She had to be right.

It was Brother Carey. It was the Brethren — all of them.

We couldn't go to the police, not after we'd turned them away when they were investigating Lord Bram's disappearance. Plus, they had been friendly with Brother Carey. And we had nothing concrete we could offer them as proof. We needed to find out more.

Half the remaining troupe stayed and kept watch over the circus grounds while the rest of us set out to search the city for clues. I was pretty sure I knew where to start looking.

All those long days when we'd been working so hard to bring our circus back to life, it had been impossible not to hear parts of Brother Carey's sermons at the edge of Carter Park.

And what had been his constant theme since the fire?

"Turn away from these wages of sin! Reject these glamorous lies and find refuge in the light and loving embrace of the Lord! Sanctuary is always granted to those who seek His mercy at our hands." And he handed out pamphlets with directions to the city cathedral on them, surrounded by further urgings to the reader to come and be saved.

It wasn't as if anyone needed directions. The cathedral's white spires needled the horizon, visible even from as far away as Carter Park. Marble and metal, all of it, white and silver and shining.

"I have to admit, it's a stunning building," I said to Tam as we approached.

"*Stunning* is the perfect word. The sight of it about whacks you on the head," fe replied.

I tried to laugh, but my fears about what might have happened to Mama and the others drowned out everything else. "I hate to think we'll find them here," I said as we walked up the wide steps leading to the cathedral's heavy double doors. "I hate it almost as much as thinking we won't find them."

The cathedral was nearly empty inside. In the aisles, a few solitary faithful said their prayers, lighting white candles and placing coins in offering boxes.

The whole place fairly gleamed with light and money.

"You can't tell me this isn't beautiful," I whispered.

"I never said it's not beautiful," Tam said, fer breath a gentle miracle against my skin. Even after the fire, after all that had happened since, just the feather-light trace of a breath was enough to make me shiver. I bit my lip, trying to pretend I wasn't wishing it were Tam doing it instead. "It's just . . . blunt," fe went on. "There's no subtlety. There aren't even any shadows — too many lights everywhere. Don't you find that . . . creepy?"

Fe was right. The intrusive brightness of the church was, in its way, more unnerving than a ghost story.

We cased the whole church and found nothing. Not that there were many places to hide in that too-bright space, anyway.

"Looking for a friend?" someone said as we walked out the front door again.

I flinched and turned. I knew that voice.

"Where are they?" I demanded.

Brother Carey served me such a blank expression that I had to admit, even then, that he could have been a top-tier performer.

And I supposed that, looking at him in his costume of black robes, standing on the white aisle of his stage, that was exactly what he was.

"If you're looking for your . . ." — he paused — "colleagues, I'd suggest that this is the last place they'd come unless they have had a true change of heart. Our doors are always open to everyone, as you can see — we would never try to turn anyone away — but unfortunately none of your group have taken my words to heart." His gaze barely flicked to Tam, who looked profoundly bored. "I'll be sure to mention your friends in my prayers, child."

I grabbed Tam's arm, and fe jumped, startled. We turned and left without another word.

"Did you see his face when he saw us?" Tam asked once we were out. "He absolutely knows something."

I frowned. "You know, Tam, there are other places in Port's End besides the cathedral that the Brethren run." As we blinked in the sunlight, something occurred to me — something so obvious that I couldn't understand how I hadn't thought of it earlier.

"What about the Houses of Light? That priest, the day you first kissed me, boasted about how they took people into the houses, young women . . ." I closed my eyes and opened them again. "The nearest House of Light is the library a few blocks away, I think."

"I have to admit," I murmured to Tam as we walked into the Sealight branch of the Brethren library system, "this place is coming much closer to converting me than the cathedral ever did."

Tam said nothing, just smiled at me. But fe didn't look away long, either, from the huge collection of books stretching from the floor to the ceiling of this place.

The library was quiet in a way the cathedral, with its high ceilings and echoing prayers, never could be. Just a few people tucked away in corners curled over their books.

"I'm wondering if Brother Carey has ever written anything. Maybe if we knew more about him, we could figure out where he's taking the people he's kidnapped," I suggested, grasping at straws.

Our search took us to the basement of the library, an area less trod, less pristine, and less full of the shiny new books that would attract the regular patrons. Here, only the historians and archivists ventured.

"I've found something!" Tam pulled a thin volume from a shelf, its leather cover embossed with Brother Carey's name in gold. Fe handed it to me.

"It looks like it's a record of his time as a missionary." I flipped through, skimming for anything that might be useful to us, until a paragraph toward the end caught my eye.

The nature of man is to cultivate bravado, a shield of belief in himself over all other forces, to hide from himself the truth of what he is and where he comes from, and it is only when he returns to his animal state that he can drop his shield and feel again the holy fear that connects him to the Lord.

As I puzzled over this, Tam moved closer to me and ran a thumb across my wrist.

I looked up at fer. Fe moved fer thumb again and a pink light twined around my skin, sending out little sparks that looked like — yes, like thorns. And just over my pulse point, the light blossomed into a delicate, transparent rose.

"It feels right," Tam murmured. Fe bent down and kissed my wrist above the bracelet. "Do you mind that I did that? I just thought — or, um, I can take it away —"

"It's perfect," I said. "I wish I could do that for you."

Fe smiled shyly. "Maybe you could make me one out of . . . a gear, say, and a leather strap," fe replied. "I've wanted to give you something for a while, but I haven't been sure how to ask you. I thought . . . I still don't feel I can stay here, Ivory, not after the contract I signed with the circus runs out. Esting still isn't a place for the Fey to feel safe, no matter what the laws say. But . . . a little light like this only takes a little corner of my mind, a little secret thought. And I'm, well, always thinking of you. And I will be, even when I leave. I want you to know that."

I reached up to bring fer in for a real kiss. If I had said anything in reply, it would have been an argument, a claim about Esting's tolerance that I'd know was not true.

Better to do something that was only what it seemed. Something I knew was real.

We were far back in the stacks by now. We'd walked through all of them, looking for secrets and clues, and we hadn't seen anyone else in a long while. Tam and I were more alone here in the recesses of the library than we ever were in the circus.

And something about books always just warms me up.

What can I say? I thought, pushing Tam up against the nearest bookshelf. *I love to learn.*

We spent, oh, the better part of an hour — the best part of any hour I've ever known — learning. Learning things about each other and putting them into practice. I learned things about Tam that I'd been longing to know for sure, and now, with hands and mouth and every part of fer body, Tam made sure that I knew.

My clothes and Tam's fluttered down around us like loose pages, some torn — that was almost definitely my fault — but even though I'd spent enough time mending costumes that I ought to have a care for my own and my performers' clothes, I really, really didn't.

I didn't care about anything except Tam's body on mine. In mine.

This — *this* — could shut off my mind, keep me from caring about anything else.

We dressed afterward in the quiet of the stacks, helping each other with buttons and ties, laughing a little as we went. There might not have been that much time to lose, but I felt as if I could breathe again, and think.

Suddenly, there were strong, strangely cool hands on me, on Tam, forcing us away from each other.

I didn't think we'd done anything wrong — at least not the way the Brethren think that anything bodies can do besides building and praying is sinful — but I had to admit that the engineering student in me felt a little bit guilty about knocking over the books that I could see splayed on the floor, pages open in such a way that they seemed naked.

I could only glare at the two Brethren who held us.

The one who had Tam, a tall, thin man with shiny brown hair, smiled coolly at me.

"The abbot has been looking for you two!" he said. "He put the word out for a dark-skinned, white-haired girl, and the speck from the circus posters. You're not exactly inconspicuous, you know."

Tam flinched at "speck," and even I was surprised to hear a priest use such crass language. It wasn't a secret that the Brethren despised the Fey, of course, but weren't they also supposed to look down on even small sins like swearing?

Not what I needed to be worried about right then. I knew the abbot was Brother Carey, and we were going to be taken to him.

As the two Brethren led us — and we let them lead, since it was clearly that or be dragged — I kept thinking that at least we had a better chance now of finding out where the others had gone.

They took us to a corner of the library basement. A swath of the wood-paneled wall swung open, and Brother Carey smiled at us from a dark stone corridor. I'd heard rumors that every House of Light was connected by underground tunnels, and I wondered if that's where we were being taken, if the tunnels ran underneath the libraries too. The priests pushed us inside and swung the heavy door back into place.

"Leave," he told them, and they obeyed immediately. He glared at the two of us as if we were insolent schoolchildren.

"Who, exactly, did you think was hunting whom?" he said. "I don't let my catches go once I have them." He looked us up and down, as if analyzing something only he could see.

"The Fey first, I think." He raised his right hand, and Tam stepped slowly forward, almost as if the gesture had compelled fer to do so.

Only magicians could compel people with a gesture, though. Brother Carey's raised hand began to glow with white light.

"Bless this sinner, O Lord, with Your second baptism."

Tam began to shake. Fe looked at me, and it seemed as if fe was struggling to reach toward me, but fer arms stayed at fer sides as if we'd been tied after all.

I tried to reach back — or I thought I tried. But it was as if my body decided it didn't want to do what my mind was urging.

Tam's blue-freckled skin turned shiny, as if only with sweat at first, and then with a metallic slickness like scales. Real scales pushed through fer skin like tiny knives, rising straight up and settling along fer skin in smooth layers. I felt heat on my wrist and at the edge of my vision I saw the light fe'd laid there turn from pink to blazing red, like an ember. But I couldn't take my eyes away from Tam.

Then fer legs drew tight together, and I heard a sickening snapping sound as fer knees bent backward. Fer legs snapped again and again, ugly bends appearing like extra sets of joints, above and below, and fe fell to the floor, fer whole body writhing, curving, curling.

Tam's face contorted in pain and scales erupted across fer

face in concentric circles, and as they closed over fer mouth, I heard fer whisper something, and I felt a sharp sting at my wrist —

And then Tam was a snake.

A dark green snake, the same length as fe had been in life, hissing on the floor.

I could suddenly reach toward fer as I'd been struggling to do through all the endless minutes as fe changed. But as soon as I did, I knew what Tam had whispered — and I looked at the band of light fe'd laid on my wrist, which had faded into a twisting, animate shadow, a darkness on my arm that spread cool energy all through my body, washing away the invisible binds the Brethren had laid on me.

And I had only moments, I knew, before Brother Carey would baptize me too.

I turned away and pushed through the door. I ran through the library, into the busy street. I don't know how I managed not to be caught, only that, as a stagehand, I am very fast when I need to be — and even better at not being noticed.

When I arrived back at the park, I was past breathlessness, past pain. I collapsed onto the drop-down stairs leading up to our caravan door.

I could hear Bear's rumbling, even, sleeping breaths from outside.

I knew Bear would not be resting unless Rosie was with him. I knew they were both still there, both still safe.

That's where Apple found me, there on the steps.

ROSIE

Bear lurches up
from sleep. My body
carries up on hers,
too sudden, waking
me up too.
She lifts her
snout to the breeze.
Nudges the gauze
from Mama's room
toward me.
The princess dreams
are close enough that I
can almost hear her voice;
but her body speaks as well.
The same smell, in the air
and on the sheets.
I look outside the caravan
to see my sister, and
Apple approaches.

IVORY

A few of the remaining stagehands trailed behind Apple. None of them seemed willing to look at me.

"Hey there, Ives," Apple said gently.

I looked up at him, still struggling to catch my breath, feeling as if my lungs must be bleeding.

But he kept standing, hands in his pockets. "Had a long day, huh?" Casual. Too calm.

I was ringmistress now, like it or not. This was no time for me to give in to my body's limits.

I swallowed my gasps as best I could, tried to turn them into breaths. I forced myself up to standing.

"What. Exactly." My voice came out as a rasp, and I had to swallow twice before I was able to form the next words. "Is wrong, Apple?"

"Don't worry too much, but —"

I glared at him, fit to kill.

"— there's more gone."

I nodded quickly, just a little. Any more movement was like to make me collapse. "How many?"

He shook his head. "Enough."

"Apple. How. Many."

He looked back toward the three small tents my wonderful Lampton classmates had managed to erect — and that I wasn't sure they'd see ever again. "There's me left, and three of the stagehands, and the dancing boys, and Bear and Rosie, and you and Tam. And the thing is, we're thinking . . ." He trailed off, pushing his hands even deeper in his pockets. He looked up at the sky. "Nice sunset, ain't it?"

Oh, this was going to be bad. Apple was only at ease when he was barking orders to the other stagehands. The more relaxed he appeared, the more he was making up for how uncomfortable he felt inside.

"The other stagehands and me, we're thinking maybe there's something to it. To what Carey and his lot have been saying."

I felt sick all over again, tired in a way I'd never felt even during this endless week.

"I mean, we have had the strangest and terriblest run of bad luck ever since we docked on these shores, and straight back from Faerie too. Maybe we brought back something that . . . Well, maybe the Brethren know something we don't. Maybe they really do know their Lord doesn't like us. Might serve us best to change with the times, slide along with what's working here. The fire alone should have been enough of a message, but our friends keep leaving —"

"The fire wasn't a message. It was just a fire. And our friends didn't leave, Apple. They were taken. Who would leave the Circus Rose? The — the family?" That word mattered to me in a way it never had before. "And leave us for the Brethren? For a life of bright light and silence and — and nothing?"

Apple looked at me seriously, and his self-conscious casualness drifted away. "I would. I am. Ives, I'm converting. So's a few others of us. The thing is, Ivory, I really feel that I've seen the light."

"Apple. The fire, the disappearances — Brother Carey is behind them."

"You don't know that, Ives," he said gently, like I was raving and he needed to mollify me.

"I do! I saw Brother Carey turn Tam into a snake! He was going to get me next, but I ran!"

"You've been under a lot of pressure, and your head's not clear. Think about it, Ives. The Brethren don't use magic." He took a deep breath. "I'm leaving now. I hope you come around. Find me if you do."

Apple doffed his hat to me and then turned to the tents and did the same thing, as if he were paying his respects in a graveyard.

One by one, the others followed.

They left. They chose to leave because they'd listened to Brother Carey, and to people like him.

And I couldn't do anything about that. I could try to rescue someone if they'd been taken against their will . . . but I'd never try to keep anyone with me who wanted to leave.

It had been so easy for the Brethren to make them decide they wanted to.

We are what's real, Mama had always said. No matter how much artifice, how much coming or going there was in circus life. *We are what's real.*

I hung my head and cried.

ROSIE

Too many gone.
Vanished. Everyone
who loved us like Mama,
every day. So
few left.
And what can I do?
What gift can I give
to those who gave me
the love I felt all
the days of my life?

Ivory's mind makes plans,
builds roads, draws maps
for how to reach
some wiser end.

What can I do?
What have I ever done?

IVORY

I was alone, all alone. Only Rosie and Bear and I remained, but Rosie had started to get closed off when she'd realized how many people were gone, and she'd had to lean on Bear as he guided her back to their bed.

Being alone wasn't what I'd dreamed it would be like. It wasn't freeing or peaceful. There is a kind of loneliness that can be precious — when you choose it.

This kind of loneliness was only grief.

I climbed the caravan steps slowly.

And went inside.

And shut the door.

There were Rosie and Bear at the back of the caravan, resting together.

I curled up with them. I didn't want my hammock or anything but the warm animal closeness of two bodies I loved next to mine.

I nestled in behind Rosie, who had her limbs wrapped around Bear in a sleeping embrace. There were no open wounds left at all, and the scars that remained, although large, already looked pinkly faded, rather than angry and red, the way Mama's scars had been at the hospital, before . . .

Before she was gone.

I'd failed her completely. Mama always said that I'd be more than able to keep the circus together if that was what I chose to do. And I'd chosen; I'd assumed her role when she couldn't —and the circus had dissolved in my hands. And it had taken nothing more than slippery words to make people believe that the thing we'd always loved was evil. With the circus under my leadership, people had chosen to leave.

No. I stopped myself. Mama, stolen from her hospital bed. Vera's blood next to Bonnie's dressing table. I had seen Tam change. Just because some had left with Apple didn't mean they all were gone. Not the ones who truly loved us and who Mama loved. I hated that I'd ever wished to be apart from them.

My circus family. I missed them so much, and I mourned them.

And by heaven and earth, I was going to get them back.

I woke up Rosie and Bear, and as we sat together outside the caravan, I talked them through the plan that was just forming in my mind as I spoke.

"Where's Tam?" Rosie leaned against my shoulder, wincing a little from the pressure on her burned arm. Bear lay down on the step behind us.

"We got caught in the library, taken to Brother Carey. He turned Tam into a snake! That must be what he's doing to everyone he takes. He would have gotten me too, but Tam used fer magic to break his hold on me long enough for me to escape."

Every muscle in Bear's body tensed up. I turned to look at his face, and it was a war zone of rage and despair. Rosie threw her arms around him, and he buried his face in her chest.

"We have to get them back."

"You're absolutely right," said a deep voice behind me.

I heard a chorus of agreement even as I turned toward the speaker. The speakers — a baker's dozen of them.

The dancing boys.

"I thought you left," I whispered.

Thirteen pairs of beautiful eyes looked at each other, all in shades of sadness and dismay.

"We listened to Apple," Ciaran said. "He deserved that much from us. But . . . we knew soon enough that there was something strange going on with him. Didn't we, boys?"

Another chorus of deep voices, the kind that would have made my knees weak before my heart leapt whole into Tam's hands.

Even now, it made me feel a little better.

Part of the family had come back. We wouldn't have to face the Brethren and Brother Carey alone.

We were never so alone as I'd wanted to be, or as I'd feared.

"I know what we're going to do," I said.

ROSIE

They think
darkness
is punishment.
Is sin.
Is separation
from the Light
of their Lord.
But I have waited
between spotlights,
slept enough sweet
nights to know

the whole show
happens backstage.

Bear scents them at once:
at the cathedral, the
white spire in the very center
of town. I can't sense

anything but incense,
but it's easy
to trust my love.

IVORY

The dancing boys walked before us through Port's End like the front guard of an army, laughing and hollering and swaying their hips and waving seductively at anyone we passed. And Ciaran led them, inviting worship with his body, drawing attention the way a butterfly draws nectar from a flower.

There were plenty of buttoned-down, startled pedestrians who gave our group strange looks — surprised, disgusted, curious, enamored, openly lustful . . .

The boys, though, they had seen it all before. They flirted madly with everyone who looked their way, and between them, they almost managed to distract the public, in the gathering gloom, from the great bear who walked in their midst, and the injured girl astride him.

Not quite. Of course not. But we looked like a traveling show, whereas with Bear alone we'd have looked like the kind of threat that could cause a panic.

Bear took us right to the cathedral.

"You're sure, now?" I whispered up toward his long black ear as we approached the heavy double doors. It was too late to change our tactic — we'd made our gambit when we started the parade — but it comforted my cautious heart to ask.

Rosie and Bear looked at each other, and Rosie nodded.

Ciaran kicked open the church doors, and we burst inside.

One of the boys had brought a flute, another castanets; they played a vibrant tune while Ciaran led the others in an exuberant dance, jumping onto the pews, twirling down the aisles, laughing and leaping up to spin around the pillars.

"What in the name of the Lord is this?" A priest bustled out of one of the side vestibules, his face pale. "Stop this sacrilege at once!"

Ciaran twirled by me, and as his handsome face passed close to mine, I saw him wink. "Go on, Ivory," he said. "We'll keep giving them a show."

Rosie and Bear had hung back near the vestibule door. As I turned to beckon them to come with me, I saw that Rosie had slipped off Bear's shoulders and stood next to him, her face more hard-set and determined than I had ever seen.

We slipped through the edges of the church, following the scent Bear caught. I couldn't help continuing to watch the boys wreak joy and celebration all over the cold white building. I thought I'd never seen anything so sacred.

ROSIE

The boys burst color
and light and song
through the near-empty church
when we arrive.
A joy in the body,
an embrace even watching them.
I'm impatient to dance again,
just seeing them, and even
I can call them gorgeous.
The priest can't look away.
The few faithful, or sinful,
who fill the front pews
stare too.

Somewhere under
this bright surface,
our family lies trapped.

Bear is going
to lead them out.

IVORY

When Bear caught the scent and led us, sure as a hunting hound, to the vestibule door, I wasn't thinking of everyone that we were going to save — I had only one person in mind. She would tell me to save the others first, but I was ringmistress now, in her absence.

And I was going to save my mama. Save Tam. Save them all.

Rosie lifted one, two fingers and slid them through the air as if she were stroking the music the dancing boys played, as if it were a cat winding invisibly around her limbs, supple and soft.

I smiled. I knew music was as dear to her as Bear.

I waited for a crescendo in the act, just as I would during a show, to hide the sounds of my footsteps. I gestured for us to move forward, and the three of us, even the huge bulk of Bear, slipped unnoticed through the door.

When it closed behind us, I heard Rosie gasp at the sudden and enveloping change in our environment. It was incredibly dark, and the stone stairs we began to descend were uneven.

"Close your eyes so they'll adjust to the dark faster," I told her in a whisper. "Hold on to Bear and me."

She took a deep breath, and I felt her strong fingers brush my back — whether in gratitude for the reminder or to find a guide in the darkness, I wasn't sure.

I never need to close my eyes. The world in darkness is just a vast backstage, and I know exactly how to manage it.

From beyond the closed door, the dancing boys' music sounded muted and underwater, and it was far easier to ignore than the blare of circus music or the rushing-ocean clamor of applause. I listened as I would for malfunctioning machinery. The next layer of sound I found was water, *drip, drip, drip*ping down from the ceiling to a pool on the unseen floor. Bear had led us this far, but I was the one who saw best in the dark, and it was my turn to lead us now.

As we wound our way down deeper underneath the church, through this narrow, damp space, I kept thinking of Brother Carey.

He never once came inside the gate of Carter Park, never bothered to see the show he so confidently denounced. Never once saw for himself what was inside.

No, he was happy enough to stand just outside and shout us down, or, when people who gave enough money to the church drew near, to speak with a lowered, polite vivaciousness. He would never deign to come inside, of course, he would tell such people. He did not see the need.

Really, I think, he was afraid.

Another door slipped open, and we breached Brother Carey's last defense, Bear, Rosie, and I.

We were there to get the others back. And I wouldn't ever wish them away again.

Even there, in the cathedral's crypt, the glaring, unfeeling light the Brethren so valued thrust its way into every corner.

Every corner of every cage.

There were dozens of animals in padlocked cages — a hundred or more. Mice and rats huddling together for warmth, many types of birds: canaries and ducks; owls and falcons and magpies; both black and gray crows. Dark, water-filled tanks, in which scores of fish sleepily lurked. Cats. Dogs. A fox, a wolf, a huge red bull, and a gray mare each in their own barred stables; a bulbous brown toad that looked at me with eyes sadder than any I'd ever seen.

And there, oh, there in a high, narrow glass terrarium — for a snake could fit through the bars of any of the cages — there was Tam. I knew fer at once.

Fe shone in a sinuous dark green coil under the gaslight, sleeping away the hours, lazily still in a way that the Tam I knew had never been, could never be.

I'd seen the change, of course, seen Brother Carey wrench fer down into this new body, but . . . I'd know Tam anywhere, in any form, whether I'd seen fer change or not. I pressed my hand to the glass, wishing I could send some warmth to the cold-blooded creature who was really the Fey I loved.

I knew I loved Tam then, in a way I had never known before, never let myself know. Because didn't I recognize fer, snake body or no? Didn't I know the heart that radiated through the skin, cool and smooth as it was?

And as soon as I knew Tam, the other animals rushed and clicked into recognition in my mind too.

Here was Toro, the man I'd towered over since I was six, turned into a great reddish bull whose hulking shoulders nearly brushed the crypt's ceiling, who could not lift his heavy head up straight for fear of lodging his horns in the soft, mealy wood beams overhead that, thanks to the Brethren's harsh lighting, I could see were beginning to swell with rot. Even the lights could not dispel the damp down here.

Here was Vera, a sweet white fluff of a little lap dog, the most innocent-looking creature in the world — had her snapping blue eyes not remained her own.

I was sure I recognized all of our circus troupe, and that feeling grew more certain when a half-grown kitten chirruped a high meow at me and I knew at once that she was Dimity, and her littermates the other Lampton girls.

The roan mare whickering next to Toro — why, that was Miss Lampton.

Bear stood frozen just beyond the doorway, looking at each of the caged animals in turn, whites showing around the edges of his dark eyes. Rosie stood with Bear, a hand over her mouth.

A lean, ginger-furred wolf seemed unfamiliar to me — plenty of the animals here were people I didn't know, just unlucky sinners who had crossed Brother Carey once too often, I was sure

— but the lion that shared the wolf's cage, his mane long and dark, and his eyes locked on me, only me . . . I knew who that was.

I knew Lord Bram. I knew my father.

I looked around — at the Lampton girls, at my circus family, at all these poor souls whom the Brethren had deprived of their bodies.

We would change them back. There had to be a way. Our two years in Faerie had shown me the promise magic held.

My heart filled with relief, but the more confident I became in seeing the human souls under those animal skins, the sicker I felt.

Because I didn't see Mama anywhere.

ROSIE

"Mama's not here," Ivory whispers, and I shake
my head in silent answer.
"We'd know it if she were," I say. "We'd know at
    once."

Neither of us say:
What is the point
of saving anyone else, if Mama is lost?

Mama, who is the center of our world,
the center of the ring,
the first beat of our waltz.

She never understood
that Ivory and I could not be a double act,
only a treble: twins and mother.

She was so grateful when Bear came,
thinking she was never enough,

always grateful that we had each other.

Not knowing where the center lay.

IVORY

I reached behind me to squeeze Rosie's hand, but my fingers brushed Bear's fur instead. His rumbling double-bass breath sent a vibration up my arm, just as comforting as it had always been when we'd snuggled on the hillock of his body in front of a campfire, Rosie and me.

As I turned to look back at Bear, smiling a little even through my fears about Mama, grateful for his constancy, his loyalty, his love —

I looked at Bear, and I saw the princess.

I saw what Rosie had seen all along.

And my heart broke — broke with shame.

· 10 ·

IVORY

My hands shook. I tore my attention away from Bear to focus on the task before me. We had to free the others before the Brethren discovered us.

I knew this, knew how to pick any lock you could present to me — locksmithing was one of the first lessons at Lampton's — but you need a steady hand, a calm heart. And those were two things, at that moment, I absolutely lacked.

I looked at Tam, trapped, and I missed fer true body so much it made my heartbeat stutter — a staccato pulse I could feel all the way out to my shaking fingertips. I could still feel fer hands on me, in me, warm ghosts haunting my body and making me shiver. And I despised Brother Carey for all he'd taken away — from Tam, from Mama, from the rest of the troupe, and from everyone he'd turned into an animal that he could keep silent and locked away and tidily labeled in this . . . this lair. For all he had taken from me.

Rosie pressed her hand quietly against the wing bone of my shoulder.

I took a shuddering breath. "Am I that badly off," I whispered, "that you're the one who has to steady me?"

Her hand rubbed a small circle on my back. "You keep pretending we haven't always been a balancing act," she murmured.

I smiled, and I found myself steadied after all.

"All right," I said. "Time for the final trick."

And before my hands had time to start shaking again, before I had any thoughts that might make them start to shake, I slipped my hairpin into the lock. I turned myself into a creature of listening, nothing more, until I heard the first click, and the next, and the last.

I pushed gently upward, and the lock opened in my hand.

Tam was free. Fer head rose slowly from the sleeping coil of fer body, and as fer eyes opened, fer black tongue feathered out, tasting the air. I saw the recognition in the snake's eyes, in Tam's eyes, that I had feared would not be there — I hadn't known I'd feared that, hadn't even let myself think about it before.

Tam slithered out of the terrarium, coiled up my arm, and draped like a boa across my shoulders. Fer length was cool, but not cold, and heavy with muscle. The smooth stroke of Tam's scales across the back of my neck was nearly as soothing as Rosie's hand.

I could feel my own skin warming the snake's, even as fer touch cooled my anguish. An exchange. A balancing act, this too.

With Tam draped around me, fer narrow head nuzzling my ear, and Rosie behind me and the great bulk of Bear behind her, my body forgot any notion of shaking. I moved to the next cage and unlocked it quickly, letting Vera out.

The white dog trotted at my side like a trained show animal, and I heard Rosie giggle behind me.

"I never thought I'd see Vera so obedient," she said just loud enough for all of us to hear.

Bear made the low rumble that is Bear's version of laughing, and Tam's black snake tongue flickered in and out a few times by my cheek. I expected a growl or a snap from Vera, but she stood up on her hind legs and made a neat little leap, then offered me her paw. A perfect circus dog—but I could see the snap of humor in her eyes too.

Rosie and Vera teasing. Tam and Bear laughing. We were coming together again. We would bring the family home, and we'd figure out how to change them back. Even if we had to go all the way back to Faerie to do it.

With every cage I unlocked, my confidence and relief grew. We would find Mama. We would fix them. No one would be abandoned. Not by me.

"Well, Lord in heaven and light on Earth."

I stopped, my hands around the melon-sized lock on Toro's cage. I knew that light, smooth voice too well—we all did.

I turned around. Brother Carey stood in the doorway in his black robes.

I'd expected that. I hadn't expected to see Apple, with the freshly shaved head of a Brethren initiate, standing next to him.

I stared, but he wouldn't meet my gaze.

"He's taking an ordeal of silence," Brother Carey said. "He showed his faith and loyalty when he helped us start the fire, and I agreed to let him take his holy orders. He made sure to warn me first, though, of just how stubborn your family is. Never willing to let anyone else have a real run of things, he said."

I saw Apple blush.

I opened my mouth to say a few choice words about Apple's silence.

But Brother Carey tugged on a thin white-gold chain at his wrist, and a drab little wren hopped out of a pocket and onto his hand. Tiny jeweled manacles linked the bird's clawed feet to Brother Carey's wrist.

I'd have known her, I was sure, even if I hadn't recognized any of the others — even Bear, who was a princess; even Tam, whom I loved.

We had found Mama.

ROSIE

When the bird sees us, she opens her beak
and tries to call, to squawk, to crow, to sing,
to make some sound — but nothing comes.

She is so silent we can hear the scrabbling
of her claws against the fine cloth on Carey's shoulder.
When the bird sees us. When Mama sees

us working to save her,
I watch as something breaks
in her bird's eyes. The feathers

sinking flat against the skin, the nestling neck
down on the downy breast. She does not look
away. She sees it all, the longing
and the need we have to save her. And I think:
I know this now. The thing I always wondered.
I see in Mama's eyes her darkest fear.

I think: *Brother Carey has broken her.*
And with her, he has broken
all of us.

Carey raises one hand, the hand that holds the chain
that binds our mama. With the other,
he searches in the pockets of his robes.

His second hand emerges
clutched around a vial
of liquid.

He begins to speak:
"Bless these, O Lord,
with Your second baptism —"

I've been holding
it back as long
as I can, but I can't,
can't. My mind a blitz.
My vision shudders,
and all I can think
is that I'm leaving her.

IVORY

Pain crept inside my body like an inverse ripple. It scraped into me anywhere it had an inlet, the corners of my eyes and mouth, my nostrils, ears, cuticles. Droplets from Brother Carey's potion hit my skin and made strange firework patterns of small holes, little gaping mouths where the change could get in, the pain of the change like sparks all over my body, like a cold burning —

What kind of animal will I become? I heard myself wondering, as if part of me were watching from far away . . .

Tam's weight on my shoulders grew heavier, until just holding fer up hurt too, and I wondered with a flinch of wild hope if somehow receiving the baptism again would change fer back.

I tried to turn my head to look and found that I could barely move it — but when I caught a glimpse of my own body, I knew Tam wasn't changing at all, wasn't getting heavier or growing.

I was shrinking.

I could feel my mind getting smaller too. All the shades of meaning I sifted through all the time, all the overthinking I chastised myself for so often, all of it was vanishing into some small point of light, perfectly and terribly bright . . .

As my thoughts and limbs shriveled in on themselves, I looked up and saw Bear charge Brother Carey.

ROSIE

My brain takes me
away to a quiet dream.
She's there. My
princess. Bear.
She tells me what she knows.
In such a soft, dark voice,
that I find my
way
back.

I wake to changes, to
animal cries
as the drops
of bright water
hit home.

Bear shields
me from the spray,

her body so many times
the size of mine.

Bear has been waiting
for her moment.

She rears on hind legs,
then leaps across the crypt,
claws drawn.

The seat of all gentleness,
the great paw where I've laid my head
since childhood,

where I have dreamed
our princess dreams,
attacks him first.
One hard blow, then another,

claws whose length
I never saw before
rake Carey's face.

The teeth come next.
He's made his own death.
Made it years ago.

Did he know
he courted it at Carter Park?

If he had ever seen Bear,
if he had come inside
to see the show,

would he have known?
If he hadn't tried
to change us too,

would Bear ever have felt
that she could
kill him?

IVORY

I was nothing, for a timeless time, but wings and a quiet song.

I knew myself to be Ivory still, but the shape of me was so small. I'd become just a bird, tucked into the coils of a snake I loved. Prey nestling into predator, the self that contained my mind too small now to make room for any animal instinct, any animal fear.

I felt Tam coil tighter around me, but only in protection. My wren's pulse fluttered against fer scales. I knew fe wouldn't let me go until we came through this, and I was glad.

More wet drops hit us, warm this time.

And while I was so small by then, and clutched in Tam's sleek length, even my bird senses knew the red drops for blood.

The blood wasn't magic. It didn't do anything to us when it hit our feathers and scales but glisten.

Yet as the blood settled, I felt a kind of release, some power gone, and I felt my mind and body grow again.

Feathers sucked into my skin, a beak pressed inside my own soft lips with a feeling like trying to swallow my teeth, pinfeathers and claws melted into nails and hair, and Tam shrank again come to the woods and sing me lullabies in secret . . ." Her eyes closed. Twin tears ran down her cheeks.

Rosie let her hair go and embraced her again, and the princess buried her face against Rosie's shoulder. When she raised her head, her pale eyelashes were thick with more tears.

"Yuliya," she said. "I always thought it was a pretty name. It's very Nordsk, I know, but I'm . . . I'm from there, after all."

And you're a princess there. I suddenly felt as if I'd stepped from the end of one story, the story of how the Circus Rose saved itself, and into the story of a lost princess named Yuliya.

I wondered if she would want to claim her kingdom now.

But there was time for that story to come. Today she had claimed her body and her name.

"It's beautiful," said Rosie. My sister placed her hands on Yuliya's cheeks, and the two girls looked into each other's eyes. There was such clarity and warmth in both of their gazes that, for a moment, it stole my breath. They shared another long kiss.

And in the firelight, all of us around them — the dancing boys, the clowns, the sword swallowers, the strongwoman, the contortionist, the Fey, the bearded lady, the engineers, and the stagehand — we all smiled.

A girl who loved a girl who used to be a bear — that wouldn't get near to top billing at the circus. It hardly even counted as strange.

I looked around the circle we made, our bodies a rim between beneath me — as I grew I shed fer body from around me as if fe were a too-small skin.

I saw Bear, mouth and claws bloody, standing over Brother Carey's corpse. I saw the broken chain at Carey's wrist that had connected him to Mama.

Apple watched us for a moment, his face twisted in terror, looking from the fallen body of Brother Carey to our changing forms. Then, before I was even myself enough to call out to him, he ran.

Who else was watching him? The room was chaos, full of transformations.

I blinked some straggling down from my eyes. My mind stretched out in its true home, and I looked around the crypt.

All the animals were changing. I heard the struggle of it: feathers shedding, fur sifting to the ground like snowfall, bodies creaking as they grew or shrank. I felt the pain of the change in the air, not just the echoes of my own — the tension of it, the way someone else's pain always pulls the air tight, so that it's hard for anyone to breathe.

I knew Brother Carey was dead. I was relieved, but I didn't want to look at him, oddly small, broken on the floor.

I would rather look at my mother, who was stretching her naked bird-wing limbs, making a strangled half cry through a beak that was already growing the dark beard I knew and loved. How it had come back after the fire had burned it away I didn't know, but the sight of it alone was enough to make me weep with joy.

At our fathers pushing out of their cage even as they changed, beastly sinews turning human in their legs and arms.

At Tam on the floor, shedding snakeskin, wincing as fe struggled to free limbs that were still stuck to fer torso as if by sutures.

I would rather look at Miss Lampton rising from all fours, stroking the horsehair on her cheek before it vanished, a look on her face as if she was lost in a memory of a horse she'd once loved.

At the Lampton girls, falling over one another with embraces as their kitten fangs receded into their gasping mouths.

At the others, so many others. The catacomb extended outward from the room we were in, and as voices began to echo through the halls, I began to wonder just how much of the city, how many of the Brethren's buildings — their churches and libraries and theaters, their Houses of Light — had underbellies that held people turned to animals. Where Brother Carey had entombed them, away from even their own bodies.

And now his death had brought them home to themselves again.

I wanted to offer all of them my help, but I remembered enough of the change — even though it already flitted, strangely buoyant and hard to capture, through some ill-fitting corner of my memory — to know that there was no help I could give, that remaking and returning to a body was something you could only do alone. That what I could do was be there for them when they had each come home into themselves.

I could see that we were changing in the order Carey had changed us: I'd healed first because I had only just turned. Tam was ferself again soon after I was, and Mama a little while after that; and one by one, the animals in the crypt recovered their human forms.

A hundred of us, at least. A menagerie of humanity. Hands that knew how to open cages.

And Bear changed last of all.

ROSIE

Bear reaches for me.
I reach for Bear. I hold
her. I will always
hold on to this love.
My scarred hands start bleeding.

Bear

starts bleeding in between
the claws, the long black stabbing claws,
Bear's blood, my blood. Both red.
I will hold on. To look at us you'd think
Bear makes me bleed, Bear hurts me,
Bear's claws invade my skin.
It is not so. It is not so.
You do not know.
This blood that's mine, this blood that's Bear's,
is not the blood of injury.

I will hold on.

I hold on.

Bear bleeds
until the claws come off.
One by one, they fall
cold, limp, and hollow on the floor,
empty as discarded toe shoes,
and the paws they leave behind,
raw skinless stubs, as red
as if they're wearing polish.
Blood painting us anew.

I look up. I know Ivory is afraid.
The smell of copper fills the room.
I try to tell her with my eyes
what we already know,
my Bear and I.
My throat is stopped and thick,
and if I spoke, I think a roar or growl would
come out.

My voice for Bear,
my skin for Bear, my blood, my life,

whatever I can give for her,
tear me open. Let it out.

We multiply.
My Bear and I,

we bleed into new bodies:
sweet bones, smooth
skin like gold dresses, burnished
and burning. Bright inside.

I give her some of what is mine.
The rest she takes from
the spell itself, I think. I hear
the princess speak to me, as if in dream
again. She takes her body back
from Carey: what he stole from her mother,
long dead.
Long dead.

Long buried
in the earth, long turned to loam,
the lining of the womb that holds the sun.

My hands grow
clean again.

My eyes, my throat,
drink in the blood, and swallow,

and open.

I know without a sound that I could sing.

I know before I look what I will see.

Bear's face is smooth, new
skin baptized with sweat.
Her bearskin circles
around her like a caul,
the remnants of the beast a crumpled gown,
hair like snow, limbs fine and curved,
graceful as she curls up
off of the floor where we bled, died,
and
rose.

So long
in this body
that its traces
litter the floor like scars.
The others, their feathers,
their scales, their fur,

are already gone. How long
it will take to vanish Bear's,
I do not know. I do
not mind. I see
her now.

Her
now.

She looks at me through sea-glass,
white-lashed eyes, my snow-white
girl. My princess.
Bear, my love.

I clasp her close and take her mouth to mine.

IVORY

Bear told us the story after.

After we escaped the crypt.

We weren't the only ones; as we emerged onto the street, I heard a hushed sound like a thousand voices whispering, a thousand feet stepping on stones. I looked behind us and saw people, mostly women, trailing out of Houses of Light all down the street, all over the city, still shaking the animals out of themselves.

Apple was not among them that I could see. I had a vague memory of his tall form running down a catacomb hall, but it was so hard to recall the things that happened while I was a bird . . .

It didn't matter. What mattered was the people who were free.

As I wondered how far the catacomb network extended, I overheard my father sharing similar thoughts with Mr. Valko and Miss Lampton.

"So many," he murmured, "a whole rotten root system. Everyone at court thought the catacombs had been closed for centuries. Who knows how long the Brethren have been using them or for what other reasons?"

"The king will deal with it," Miss Lampton said, "and well. You'll see. He removed the Brethren from the government as soon as he was coronated, and he'll root them out again."

"I hope so," Mr. Valko said. "I'd like to think Port's End could be a safe place for our family, if . . ."

He clasped my father's hand.

I pushed ahead, found Mama, and clasped hers.

Bear told us her story after.

After we were back in Carter Park.

After Mama, her burn scars vanished since she'd come back to herself, insisted on starting a new campfire.

After Bear and Rosie managed to stop kissing.

Which, in itself, took a long time.

And Rosie still nestled on Bear's lap even as she talked — and it was strange to see the change between them. Bear was tall, as most of the Nordsk were, but she was thin and weak, as if she'd never used her human muscles before — which, I supposed, she hadn't. Sturdy acrobat Rosie was shorter, but she still looked like a bigger girl than Bear.

Bear, who was a princess.

"I feel like I should . . . curtsey to you, or some such," I'd told her shyly as we'd made our way back to the park. "It feels as strange now as it did when you were . . . well, when I thought you were . . ."

The princess had stopped me with a long, elegant, unearthly soft finger pressed to my lips.

"What is your name?" Tam asked her now.

The question stunned the rest of us silent, it was so obvious. How had none of us thought to ask?

The princess shook her head, and her long silvery hair spilled over her face. She tucked it back with a slender hand, fumbling over the shape of her own skull.

Rosie stroked her hair, smiling, and started to braid it.

"My mother never gave me one," she said. "I was born a bear. I was changed in the womb, as a curse on her. She didn't want to name me when she saw my body."

"The matinee," Tam murmured.

I was sitting in front of Tam, leaning back against fer with fer arms around me and fer legs on either side of my hips, and I glanced back at fer, surprised. "What?"

"The play in the Brethren theater. The woman running away, the priest, the bear . . ."

I remembered the animatronic beast I'd barely glimpsed as Tam led me out. I was sure the version of the story told in a Brethren-sponsored play would be very different from Bear's version, but I thought I could imagine it well enough.

"My mother was a Nordsk queen, an unmarried ruler of a very small and wild kingdom. We had our own beliefs there, once, before the Brethren came. They converted my grandparents the same way they tried to do in Faerie" — she nodded at Tam — "and they tried to convert my mother. She resisted at first. Then she became pregnant out of wedlock, and the Brethren decided to make an example of her. One of their priests cursed me in her womb and told her that her unmaidenly behavior meant that I would be no maid myself, but a beast.

"I was her burden, you see, from the minute I was born. She couldn't stand the sight of me and sent me to live in the woods, with a real bear, as soon as she could."

Bear fell silent, overcome, recounting the loss of her mother.

Rosie took up the story.

"Bear had always known she was a princess and a girl. And she'd felt drawn to the circus, all those years ago, after watching the bright glow of us from the wilderness, wanting to be part of it but still not knowing why she came until she met us, Mama, Ivory. Until she . . . met me. I saw her in my dreams sometimes or when I . . . went to that place in my head where I go. The princess. We didn't speak much, in our dreams, but I came to know her."

I swallowed painfully.

"Bear found us, and she loved us, and she loves us. And we love her." Rosie laid small delicate kisses along the braid she was making. "And I love her."

They smiled at each other, so full of sweetness that my heart both ached and soared.

"Do you want us to call you Bear still?" I asked.

The princess frowned thoughtfully for a moment, then smiled. "No. I think . . . I think I'd like to name myself. There was a woman, one of my mother's ladies in waiting, who used to nighttime darkness and firelight. Our circus family was smaller by one, but we had grown by six, since Miss Lampton and the girls were still here.

And perhaps it would soon grow by two more. I watched Mama, across the fire with our fathers, their arms around each other's shoulders.

It still hurt, not to know what to expect. Not to be able to be sure of them.

But then, I was learning to be all right with uncertainty.

I was starting to think I might go back to Lampton's next term. I still wore Tam's glowing rose on my wrist, and it had made me feel sure about something in a way I never had been before: that I didn't have to prove love with my presence. That I wouldn't be leaving anyone lonely by *leaving*, for a while. That Mama, and even Rosie, would be all right without me. That I didn't have to stage-manage our lives anymore.

Tam would leave too. Soon. Fer contract was always going to end when the season was over.

I knew that I wouldn't ask fer to make plans or promises beyond that. We didn't have to prove anything to each other. That uncertainty, at least, was sweet; it felt like freedom, and it let me be a little more generous with Mama too.

Her ring was still waiting in the drawer where I'd left it in the caravan. And if she still wanted it, if she still wanted one or both of our fathers — and from the way the three of them leaned against each other, it seemed they all wanted one another — I was glad of it. Glad for all of them.

Besides, there was a radiant glow coming from my beautiful sister and her princess, suffusing the whole circus grounds with a sweet blossoming that filled everyone's hearts up at once, just looking at them — at a love we all should have seen coming.

One happily-ever-after was more than enough that night.

I pulled on the leather cords I was knotting into the bracelet Tam had asked for. As I worked, fe leaned over and brushed fer lips against my neck. My eyes fluttered closed and then open again.

Tam. Mama. Rosie. Yuliya. Vera and Toro, Ciaran, Bonnie, Miss Lampton, Dimity and the girls, the rest of the troupe, and our fathers too. I could see the animal forms flickering still in those who had changed — what they had been, the knowledge that they, that we, were never only what we seemed. And I was glad of it.

I leaned back into Tam, letting myself feel the strength and the softness in fer arms as fe held me. I closed my eyes and whispered:

"We are what's real."

ACKNOWLEDGMENTS

I wrote *The Circus Rose* during a particularly precarious high-wire act in my life, as I transitioned into single parenthood. I want to thank a few people without whom I wouldn't have had the time, resources, or fortitude to finish this manuscript: Anna Boarini, Susan Burke and the Cox family, Trish Connolly, Josephine Fahy, Leah Gilbert, Danielle Hall, Joan and John Harte, Anne Jarrett, Eleanor Lane, Zoë Langsdale, Aoife Light, Kathrin Sauter, Anjelika Vayas, Natalia Yepez-Frias, Alex Zaleski, the survivors' group at Waterside House in Galway, and the members of Friday Tea in the Cloud. I am lucky to know you.